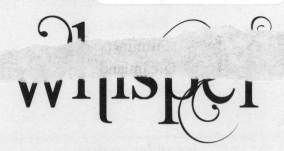

Whisper

Alyson Noël is the author of many books for teens, including the bestselling The Immortals series. Her books have been published in thirty-five countries and have sold millions of copies around the world. She lives in California, where she's busy working on her next novel, but her favourite city is Paris. If Alyson could travel back in time she'd visit Renaissance Florence, but only if she could take her modern-day grooming habits! Alyson is an eternal optimist, who always believes in silver linings.

The Riley Bloom series

Radiance

Shimmer

Dreamland

Whisper

For older readers

The Immortals series

Evermore

Blue Moon

Shadowland

Dark Flame

Night Star

Everlasting

The Soul Seekers series

Fated

Echo

Mystic

Horizon

www.AlysonNoel.co.uk

ALYSON NOËL

Whisper

MACMILLAN

First published in the US 2012 by Square Fish, an imprint of Macmillan

This edition published in the UK 2012 by Macmillan Children's Books
a division of Macmillan Publishers Limited
20 New Wharf Road, London N1 9RR
Basingstoke and Oxford
Associated companies throughout the world
www.panmacmillan.com

ISBN 978-1-4472-0047-5

1 3 5 7 9 8 6 4 2

A CIP catalogue record for this book is available from
the British Library.

Printed and bound by CPI Group (UK) Ltd, Croydon CR0 4YY

For you.

Yes, YOU.

The one holding this book.

Thank you for taking this journey with Riley and me!

"None of us will ever accomplish anything excellent or commanding except when he listens to this whisper which is heard by him alone."—Ralph Waldo Emerson

Residual Haunting Thought to be the most common form of haunting where a ghost re-enacts a repetitive routine with no awareness of anyone or anything outside of that routine.

I

The first thought that popped into my head when we entered the Roman city limits was: *Hunh?*

I squinted into the wind, droopy blond hair streaming behind me, feeling more than a little deflated as I soared over a landscape that was pretty much exactly the same as all the others before it.

My guide Bodhi, my dog Buttercup, and I had flown a great distance to get there, and even though flying was hands down our favorite way to travel, there was no denying how after a while the scenery tended to get a bit dull—fading into a continuous blur of clouds, and nature, and man-made things, all piled up in a row. And though I'd grown used to it, I guess I still hoped that Rome would be different, but from where we hovered, it all looked the same.

Bodhi turned to me, his green eyes taking note of my disappointed face, he shot me a quick grin and said, "Follow me."

He thrust his arms before him and somersaulted into a major free-fall as Buttercup and I did the same. And the faster we spun toward the earth, the more the landscape below came to life—blooming with such vibrant color and detail, I couldn't help but squeal in delight.

Rome wasn't boring. It was more like the opposite—a city chock-full of visual contradictions practically everywhere you looked. Consisting of a maze of crazily curving, traffic-choked streets that curled and swooped around newly renovated buildings and crumbling old ones—all of it looming over dusty old ruins dating back thousands of years—reminders of a long ago history that refused to go quietly.

Bodhi slowed, his hair flopping into his face when he nodded toward the ruin just below him and said, "There it is. What do you think?"

Buttercup barked with excitement, wagging his tail in a way that made him spin sideways, as I gawked at the massive old amphitheater, marveling at its size, and finding myself suddenly sideswiped by doubt.

I mean, yes, I'm the one who'd practically begged the Council for a more challenging Soul Catch—I wanted to glow brighter, wanted to turn thirteen more than anything else in the world, and I wrongly believed that excelling at my job was the one and only way to speed that along. But the longer I gazed upon that massive stone structure with its arching columns and sturdy old walls—the more I took in its sheer size and scope—the more I thought about the activities it was known for: barbaric cruelty and slaughter, blood-soaked battles fought to the death—well, I couldn't help but wonder if I'd maybe been a little too ambitious, if I might've overreached.

Not wanting to let on to my sudden fit of cowardice, I gulped hard and said, "Wow, that's um . . . that's a whole lot bigger than I thought it would be."

Continuing to hover, my eagerness to land all but forgotten until Bodhi yanked hard on my sleeve and got us all moving again. But instead of leading us to the middle of the arena, he landed on the balcony of a very fancy restaurant, its all-white décor serving as the perfect backdrop to what may be one of the earth plane's most spectacular views.

He perched on the balcony's gray iron railing, gazing down at the landscape that loomed several stories below, while I sat alongside him, hoisting a not-so-cooperative Buttercup awkwardly onto my lap, his legs flopping over either side, as I said, "Do we have a dinner reservation I don't know about?" Knowing the joke was a dumb one, but I couldn't help it, nerves made me jokey.

Bodhi gave the place a once-over, taking in the spacious terrace filled with well-dressed diners enjoying elegant candlelit dinners and a sunset-drenched view that bathed the Colosseum in a glow of orange and pink—all of them blissfully unaware of the three ghosts sitting among them.

Then returning to me he got down to business and said, "Okay, here's the deal, this ghost you're supposed to deal with—his name is Theocoles. No last name that I know of. And, please, do yourself a favor and call him by his *full* name. No shortcuts, no Theo, or T, or Big T, or—"

"I got it, Theocoles," I snapped, thinking it was certainly a mouthful but it's not like it mattered, his name was pretty much the least of my concerns at that point. "What else?" I stared straight ahead, hoping to appear confident despite the way my fingers were twisting in Buttercup's pale yellow fur.

Bodhi squinted through his heavy fringe of thick lashes, his voice low and deep as he said, "According to the Council, he's been haunting the Colosseum for a very long time." I turned to Bodhi, arching my brow, in need of a little more detail, watching as he shrugged, pulled a dented green straw from his pocket and shoved it into his mouth, where he proceeded to gnaw on it. A habit meant either to calm his nerves or help him think, I could never be sure. "This guy is *intense*," he continued. "He truly is a lost soul. He's so completely immersed in his world, he has no concept of anything outside of it, or just how many years have passed since his death, which, by the way, number into the thousands."

I nodded, giving Buttercup one last scratch on the head before allowing him to leap from my lap to the ground so he could go sniff all the diners and beg for table scraps—clueless to the fact that they couldn't see him.

"Sounds like business as usual," I replied, with a little more bravado than I felt. While the Colosseum was certainly intimidating, nothing Bodhi had said sounded like all that big a deal. "Pretty much all the ghosts I've dealt with were intense," I continued. "And yet I was still able to reach them, still able to convince them to cross the bridge and move on, so I'm pretty sure I can convince this Theocoles dude to cross over too. Easy-peasy." I nodded hard to confirm it, turning just in time to catch the wince in Bodhi's gaze.

"There's something more you need to know," he said, his voice quiet and low. "Theocoles was *the* champion gladiator back in his day. Feared by all—defeated by none."

"Did you say . . . *gladiator*?" I gaped, thinking surely I'd misunderstood.

Bodhi nodded, quick to add, "They called him the Pillar of Doom."

I blinked, tried to keep from laughing, but it was no use. I know the name was supposed to sound scary, but to me it sounded like some silly cartoon.

My laughter fading the second Bodhi shot me a

concerned look and said, "He was a *champion* gladiator. A real *primus palus*, that's what they called them, which, just so you know, translates to *top of the pole*. Widely considered to be the toughest, scariest, strongest, most fearless creature in the bunch. This is nothing to laugh about, Riley—I'm afraid you've got some serious work cut out for you. But then again, you did beg for a challenge."

My shoulders slumped as I buried my face in my hands, my short burst of confidence dying the moment the reality of my situation sank in.

I mean, seriously—a *gladiator*? That's the challenge the Council saw fit to assign me?

It had to be a trick, or maybe even some kind of joke.

It had to be the Council's way of getting back at me for always ignoring their rules in favor of making my own.

How could I—a skinny, scrawny, semi-stubby-nosed, flat-chested, twelve-year-old girl—how could I possibly take on a big, strong, raging hulk of a guy who'd spent the better part of his life chopping his competition into small, bloody bits?

Just because I was dead—just because he couldn't technically harm me—didn't mean I wasn't quaking with fear. Because I was—I really, truly was. And I'm not afraid to admit it.

"I know it seems like a lot to ask of a fairly new Soul

Catcher such as yourself," Bodhi said. "But not to worry, the Council only assigns what they know you can handle. The fact that you're here means they believe in you, so it's time you try to believe in you too. You have to at least try, Riley. What is it Mahatma Gandhi once said?" He looked at me, pausing as though he actually expected me to provide the answer, and when I didn't he said, "*Full effort is full victory.*" He paused again, allowing the words to sink in. "All you can do is give it your best shot. That's all anyone can ever ask of you."

I sighed and looked away. Believing in myself was not something I was used to struggling with—if anything I bordered on dangerously overconfident. Then again, the situation I faced wasn't the least bit normal, or usual for that matter. And even though I knew I'd asked, if not begged for it, I still couldn't help but resent the Council just the tiniest bit for indulging me.

"And what about those other Soul Catchers?" I asked. "The ones who were sent before me and failed? I'm assuming the Council believed in them too, no?"

Bodhi chewed his straw, ran a nervous hand through his hair, and said, "Turns out, it didn't end so well for them . . ."

I squinted, waiting for more.

"They got lost. Sucked so deep into his world that they . . ." He paused, scratched his stubble-lined chin, and took his sweet time to clear his throat before he said, "Well, let's just say they never made it back."

I stared, my mouth hanging open, empty of words.

I was outmatched. There was no getting around it. But at least I wouldn't have to go it alone. At least I had Bodhi and Buttercup to serve as my backup.

"But please know that Buttercup and I will be right here if you need us. We're not leaving without you, I promise you that."

I looked at him, my eyes practically popped from their sockets, my voice betraying the full extent of my hysteria when I said, "You expect me to go in *alone*?" I shook my head, unable to believe how quickly things had gone from very, very bad to impossibly worse. "I thought that as my guide it was your job, not to mention your duty, to *guide* me. And what about Buttercup? Are you seriously telling me that I can't even bring my own dog to protect me?"

I turned, gaze sweeping the restaurant until I'd zeroed in on my sweet yellow Lab all crouched under a table, chewing on a shiny gold stiletto a diner had slipped off her foot. Reminding myself that historically speaking, he'd never proved to be all that great of a backup, when push came to shove he was actually more scaredy-cat than menacing guard dog— but still, he was loving, and loyal (well, for the most part), and surely that was better than going alone.

Bodhi looked at me, his voice full of sympathy when he said, "Sorry, Riley, but the Council made it crystal clear that this was *your* Soul Catch. Yours and yours alone. They asked me to stay out of it, to supervise only, and leave you to work it out on your own. But we'll try to throw you a lifeline if you need it—or should I say *soul-line*? And while I thought about letting you bring Buttercup along, for the company if nothing else, the thing is, thousands of wild animals died in that arena, and some of them are still lurking in ghost form. Being chased by a lion or bear could be pretty terrifying for him since he doesn't really get that he's dead."

I squinted into the dying light, gazing at the long, rect-angular space filled with rows of narrow, crumbling, roofless structures all sprawled out below us—yet another ancient ruin. From what I'd seen, Rome had no shortage of them.

"It'll be dark soon," Bodhi said, voice softly nudging. "The sooner you get started, the better—and you might want to start there." He gestured toward the ruin I'd been looking at. "It's an ancient *ludus*—the Ludus Magnus—known as one of the biggest, most important gladiator schools in Rome's history. Could be a good place to begin, get your bearings, get a feel for the place . . . you know, before you hit the arena."

The arena.

I gulped, nodded, tried not to think about my fellow

Soul Catchers who never made it back. I mean, if the Council thinks I can handle it, well, who knows, maybe I can? Maybe they know something I don't.

I pushed my bangs from my face, took one last look at my dog still gnawing that shoe, then pushed off the ledge. Hoping more than anything that the Council was right, that I really was capable of more than I thought.

But already betting against it as I made my way down.

2

The first thing I noticed when I landed in the *ludus* was the noise. It was loud. Insanely, annoyingly loud. So loud I was unable to sift through it, unable to determine which world it belonged to—the physical, the unearthly, or both.

The second thing I noticed was the smell. Just because I was dead—just because I no longer breathed—didn't mean I couldn't smell. And that particular smell, well, it was awful—unbearable, revolting, and putrid in the very worst way. Like all the worst smells in the universe had been blended together and pumped into the very spot where I stood.

I moved, hoping to find someplace quiet, desperate to get a whiff of something a little more pleasant. My shoes alternately slip-slopping through the mud and skidding over large patches of weeds still damp from the morning rain, as

I tried to get a better look at the same crumbling ruins I'd seen from above. But all I could make out was soggy earth, crumbling walls, and . . . well . . . that's about it. There were no people, no ghosts, no wild animals—neither living nor dead, and absolutely no reason whatsoever for why it should smell so horribly foul.

I glanced back toward Bodhi, half expecting to find him and Buttercup perched at a table, enjoying their own elegant five-course meal, having totally forgotten about me—and relieved to find Bodhi still balancing on the railing right where I'd left him. Smiling and waving and urging me on, sending me a telepathic message that quickly wound its way to my head.

Don't worry. The reassuring sound of his voice swirled deep within me. *You can do this. Just ask yourself: What's the one thing most ghosts share in common?*

I paused, hooked my thumbs into my blue denim belt loops, and thought long and hard. Cracking a smile when I replied: *Terrible fashion sense?* Remembering some of the truly horrendous ensembles some ghosts chose to wear, despite the fact that they were perfectly capable of manifesting just about anything else.

Bodhi laughed. I was hoping he would. It broke up the tension and helped me relax. *Well, yeah, there is that,* he replied. *But what does that horrible fashion sense prove?*

It took me less than a second to get it, and, unfortunately for Bodhi, my answer must've sounded like a shout in his head: *It proves that they're stuck! It proves that they're stuck in the time that they died in and refuse to move on!*

Exactly ☺, he confirmed, adding a smiley face to go along with it—a telepathic emoticon that made me smile too. *They're stuck, and Theocoles is no different. He doesn't experience the ludus in the same way as you. So far, you've only skimmed the surface. In order to see what he sees, you have to go deeper. You have to see it as it used to be. Though I'm afraid my guidance ends here, I'm not allowed to tell you how to do that.*

I frowned, wondering if it was the Council who forbade him from helping me, or if he came up with that all on his own. Bodhi was never much for giving away the tricks of the Soul Catcher trade, or any other kind of helpful hints or advice that might actually help me do my job. Everything I'd learned so far, I'd learned on my own, the hard way—through trial and error and hands-on experience. And while he still hadn't told me anything I didn't already know, maybe that's exactly what a good guide does—reinforces the knowledge you've already learned.

I froze, shocked by the words that replayed in my head.

I'd referred to Bodhi as a *good* guide.

Practically from the moment we'd met I'd been

petitioning for his replacement. All we ever seemed to do was fight and bicker and argue—only agreeing to work together when we were knee-deep in trouble and all out of options.

Which is why I couldn't fathom my sudden change of heart. Where had it come from? At what point had I stopped seeing him as my number one enemy?

And then I remembered. Remembered the day I'd seen him with his new girlfriend Jasmine. Remembered how strange it made me feel to watch him read poetry to her, pausing a moment to manifest a flower—a jasmine for Jasmine—that he gently weaved into her braids.

I shook my head, ridding myself of the thought. I had a big, bad gladiator ghost to deal with, and wasting time thinking about my ever-evolving relationship with Bodhi wasn't going to change that. So I returned my attention to the *ludus*, knowing I had to find a way to see it in the same way Theocoles did if I had any chance of meeting him. Problem was, I had no idea how those crumbling old walls might've looked in his day. I'd died well before my History class got around to studying the Roman Empire.

I continued to pace, trying to see it in the way it once stood. Manifesting a roof, replacing the bed of weeds with a dry, dirt floor—but sadly that's about the best I could do. I mean, excuse me for saying so, but I died in the twenty-first century—a child of the new millennium. Recreating an ancient gladiator school was a little out of my league.

I gritted my teeth, pushed my scraggly bangs off my face, and vowed to try again. Noticing a small pile of rocks that shone like bones in the moonlight, I bent to examine them—tracing my fingers over their deep crags and crevices, I closed my eyes and thought: *What am I missing? Please show me—show me everything there is to see!* And when I opened my eyes and looked all around, I couldn't help but gasp in surprise.

The universe had answered my wish.

But instead of finding myself face-to-face with Theocoles, I found myself surrounded by hundreds of angry, raging gladiator ghosts.

3

I cowered in the dirt, my arms circling protectively as I lowered my head to my knees, attempting to make myself smaller, less of a target, doing my best to avoid the rampage of angry ghosts. Punching the air with their fists, they shouted and roared a long list of threats at some unseen enemy—the words spoken in a language that, much like them, had died centuries before, though the message rang clear. Every last one of them so consumed by their memories, they were blind to everyone else.

Spying an opening in the crowd, I jumped to my feet, only to be knocked down again by a huge, hulking monster of a ghost who thundered right past me. Not even bothering to stop or slow down when his shoulder plowed smack into my jaw.

"Hey—watch it!" I yelled, rolling my eyes and shaking my head as I struggled to my feet once again. "I mean, I get that you're like a gazillion times bigger than me, but do you really have to be so *rude*?"

I scowled, thrust my hands on my hips, and glared at his retreating back. Willing him to turn and give me the apology he most certainly owed me, but he just kept going, as oblivious to my presence as he was to the noise that blared all around. A noise that was not only loud and unpleasant, but also, or at least in the beginning anyway, impossible to make out. Though it wasn't long before I was able to break it into more manageable chunks. Instantly recognizing it as the sound of hunger and pain and uncontrollable rage—in other words, the sound of enslavement, I'd heard it before.

It was continuous. Unceasing. The only relief coming in a quick burst of laughter that ended as soon as it started. Though I couldn't imagine what could possibly be worth laughing about in that horrible underground prison of sorts.

Brushing the dirt from my jeans, I set off. Having seen just enough of the *ludus* to know I didn't want to linger any longer than I had to, I was more determined than ever to get down to the business of finding Theocoles so I could cross him right over and get the heck out.

Though finding the champion gladiator was not nearly as easy as I'd thought, mostly because I didn't have much of a description to go on. What little Bodhi had told me—*big, strong, tough, scary, intense*—amounted to no more than a generic stream of words that could be easily applied to any one of the ghosts that haunted the place.

At first glance, they all looked the same. A bunch of overly muscled, filthy, dirty, greasy-haired men who'd been sliced apart and sewn back together so many times their skin resembled a cheap leather purse. Each of them bearing a pair of hands that were so big and meaty and brutal-looking, they could easily kill with a flick of a wrist.

It was like a never-ending parade of warriors, one fearless fighter after another. And just when I'd started to separate them as individuals, one would shift, I'd quickly lose track, and they'd all blur together again.

I guess I'd been so focused on dealing with Theocoles that it never occurred to me there'd be so many other lost souls lingering in the *ludus* as well. Though I should've known since most ancient sites that played host to horrendous acts of violence and repression were known to be haunted by angry spirits demanding justice before they'd move on.

I slunk around the place, at first keeping close to the walls, doing my best to stay inconspicuous, stay out of the way, assuring myself that if I could just steer clear of the jab-bing elbows and swinging fists, it would all be okay. Making my way down the corridor, I poked my head into a series of small, narrow rooms I guessed to be the gladiators' bed-rooms. Though unlike my own recently redecorated room back in the Here & Now, which consisted of every modern comfort and convenience I could dream of (and I mean that literally since I manifested everything in it)—these were pretty much the opposite—pretty much the definition of *bleak*. Consisting of dirt floors, severe wooden bed frames that were shoved against either wall, and, well, not much else. Though, not surprisingly, the rooms were all empty.

That's the thing with ghosts—they don't really sleep, and they pretty much always refuse to rest. They're way too caught up in reliving their pasts to make time for any sort of leisure activity like that, and these ghosts were no different. Prowling the halls, yelling and screaming—it seemed like the more I looked, the more their numbers grew, leaving me to wonder if I'd ever locate Theocoles among the restless swarm.

Knowing I had to start somewhere, I began tugging on tunics and poking at elbows, each time asking the exact same question: *Do you know where I can find Theocoles, the one they call the Pillar of Doom?*

And each time getting the exact same reply: a blank-eyed stare, which only confirmed what I already knew—I was pretty much invisible as far as they were concerned.

I turned a corner, made my way down a series of short corridors, and had just began trudging down another when I froze in my tracks. Gasping in horror when I found myself standing in the doorway of a room so grisly I had to clamp a hand over my mouth just to keep from screaming.

I peered into the dark, my eyes moving from the rough, bloodstained walls to the heap of severely wounded gladiators who lay on old, splintered planks. Their bodies thrashing against the thick, iron shackles that imprisoned their ankles and wrists—moaning and grumbling and howling in pain—a chorus of agony so awful, I couldn't help but shiver in fear.

It was a torture chamber—an ancient house of horrors— of that I was sure. Though it wasn't long before my eyes adjusted and I saw I'd misread the whole thing—it wasn't that at all.

It was a hospital, an infirmary, an ancient sanatorium run by a man I guessed to be the doctor, or medic, or whatever they called them back in the day. And I couldn't help but cringe as I watched him tend to the gladiators' wounds with a bizarre array of pastes and salves and other grotesque concoctions that smelled even worse than the infections that oozed out of them.

Still, even though he did his best to heal them, to my eyes it remained a scene lifted straight from a horror movie—a scene I was desperate to flee. Bolting as fast as I could, I tackled the stairs two at a time, pushing my legs beyond all reasonable limits, wishing there was a way to outrun the shocking images that blazed in my mind.

Finally reaching the landing, I paused against a sturdy stone column that fronted an open, shade-covered room that, judging by the number of gladiators sitting on long wooden benches, hunched over shallow wooden bowls, greedily slurping some kind of horrible, lumpy, gray porridge, I guessed it to be a cafeteria. And while unlike the hospital, there was no blood and gore, it was still pretty gruesome in its own way, leaving me to wonder, yet again, at the logic of some of these ghosts. I couldn't even begin to fathom why anyone would ever willingly choose to stay in such a gawd-awful place.

Spying the practice arena just a few feet beyond, I made my way toward it. My hand pressed to my forehead, shielding myself from the sudden rush of heat and glare, I took a good look around, noting how just like the barracks, the hospital, and the cafeteria before it, it was also crowded with spooks.

Their long, wooden practice swords sliced through the air, as their round wooden shields jabbed and punched at some unknown opponent before them. My eyes darting furiously, searching for Theocoles among them, figuring if he was to be found anywhere in this *ludus* it would be here. As the undefeated champion, it just seemed to make sense.

Problem was, I was so clueless as to how it all worked, it

was impossible to tell who was the best one among them—the one good enough to be champion—the one worthy of being called the Pillar of Doom—when they all looked so determined, so fearless, so eager to destroy whatever unlucky opponent stood in their way. All of them sharing that same ruthless eagerness to kill, to slaughter, to shred and destroy—burning like a flame in their eyes.

I was just about to give up, just about to head over to the Colosseum and try my luck there, when I saw something so unexpected, I forced myself to blink a few times to make sure it wasn't a mirage of some sort—make sure I hadn't somehow dreamed it all up.

It was a girl.

A beautiful dark-haired girl standing on a balcony that overlooked the arena.

The only other girl in the place besides me.

Though unlike me, she was dressed in a way that was far more appropriate to the time. While I was in jeans, a (super-cute) tee, and my favorite ballet flats, she wore a gorgeous silk gown that draped and swirled and trailed over the ground.

I studied her closely, taking in her smooth olive skin, her sweep of long, glossy, dark hair—the front of which was fastened at the crown by a shiny jeweled clasp, while the rest was left to tumble over her shoulders and down to her waist in a riot of waves.

Running a hand down the front of her elaborate red gown, she focused hard on the gladiators below. Her long, slim fingers picking at the embroidered gold sash at her waist, looking so elegant, so beautiful, so graceful and refined, I couldn't even begin to imagine what she might be doing in such a sad, filthy place.

Or at least that's what I thought until I looked a little closer and noticed how she focused on one gladiator in particular. The intensity of her gaze telling me he was someone special, not just to her, but to the arena in general.

I followed the length of her flashing brown gaze, my eyes lighting on a gladiator who rose above all the rest. He was taller, stronger, his movements both brutal and graceful.

He was a savage fighter. There was no doubt in my mind. But unlike the others who grunted, and punched, and kicked up great clouds of dust, this gladiator was different.

This one had the poise, and presence, and arrogance that could only belong to a champion.

And I knew in that instant, I'd just found Theocoles.

4

While I'd been told more than once that I possessed all the delicacy and finesse of a bull in a china shop, as far as Theocoles was concerned, I was determined to take an entirely different approach.

Which is to say that I didn't approach him at all.

Instead I approached the girl I'd seen watching him.

Or at least I tried to approach her. Though the truth is I didn't get very far. The moment she saw me grinning and waving from the space just below where she stood, she vanished. Just *poof* and she was gone. But not before I caught the look of pure shock displayed on her face.

Unlike the others, she'd seen me. And at that point, with not much else to go on, it felt like progress. It felt like a start.

I wound my way past the gladiators, ducking and dodging around their fiercely punching swords—stopping beside the one the girl had been watching, wondering why I'd failed to notice him before.

From this angle he was even taller than I'd first thought. He towered a good foot above the rest, which is probably why he didn't look nearly as bulky. Though that's not to say he wasn't strong, because he was. The circumference of just one bicep alone appeared wider than both my legs put together. And while his skin bore its fair share of battle scars, it was nothing excessive, or at least not compared to what I'd seen on his fellow fighters.

He dropped his sword to the ground and wiped a hand across his brow, clearing it of the heavy sheen of sweat that shone on his forehead, while sweeping aside the tangle of long dark curls that fell into his eyes. Revealing a face that, aside from a nose that had clearly been broken once or twice, was dark and smooth and surprisingly unblemished for someone in his line of work. And I couldn't help but think that in another time and place—a more modern time and place—he would've been splashed across magazine covers and movie screens. But in ancient Rome, his fame was due solely to the grisly acts he'd committed with his sword.

Sensing I had only seconds to spare before he returned to his drills, I was just about to speak when he turned to me with eyes the color of deep gleaming topaz, causing the speech I'd prepared to sputter and spurt into an embarrassing garbled up mess that went something like: "Um, hi. Excuse me for bothering you." I waved my hand back and forth in a lame attempt at friendliness. "But would you happen to be Theocoles . . . uh, you know . . . the one they call the Pillar of Doom?"

He grunted, cleared his throat, and had the audacity to hock a big fat loogie directly at me.

A big fat loogie that landed in the exact same spot where I'd stood just seconds before I gasped and jumped out of the way.

I glared between him and the puddle of *ick,* shouting, "How *dare* you!" I shook my head, felt my cheeks grow red. "I mean, seriously! While I get that you're from another, far more *barbaric* time in history—while I get that because of that we may not be on the same page where manners are concerned—still, you cannot tell me that you truly don't realize just how incredibly rude that was!"

He stooped toward the ground, scooped a mound of dirt into his hands, and rubbed it into his palms before retrieving his sword and wiping the handle as well. Acting like he didn't see me. Acting like he hadn't just totally insulted me in the very worst way.

I was just about to really let him have it, when a soft voice drifted from behind me and said, "I'm afraid he cannot hear you."

I turned to find the girl from the balcony.

"Neither can he see you. So please, do not take offense." She glanced between the gladiator and me. "Theocoles sees only what he chooses to see. You and I are invisible to him."

I frowned. Scowled. Slewed my gaze first his way then hers, saying, "From what I can tell, I'm invisible to everyone but you. What gives?"

I folded my arms across my chest and gave her a thorough once-over, unable to keep from noticing how her nearness only seemed to magnify just how different we were. And though I tried not to feel small, and insignificant, and completely outclassed by her presence, it was no use.

She was tall—I was puny.

She was pretty—I was forced to settle for cute.

She was curvy and girly—I was skinny, scrawny, and as shrimpy as it gets.

And even though her clothes were completely outdated, there was no denying her gorgeous red gown definitely worked in her favor.

There was no getting around it—she completely and totally eclipsed me in every conceivable way. She was a bright, shining star, while I was a planet so small and insignificant it had never been named.

My thoughts interrupted by the lilt of her voice saying, "Unfortunately, those you see here are as enslaved in their afterlives as they were in their physical lives." She paused, her perfect pink mouth pulling into a frown. "They refuse to let go and move on."

I quirked a brow in response, it's not like she'd just revealed something new. If anything, it was just the same ole same ole—definitely a scenario I was all too familiar with. All of the ghosts I'd met so far had been enslaved by their lives and unwilling to let go of their pasts—and believe me, they all claimed to have a very good list of reasons for choosing to linger. Not unlike me back when I was haunting the earth plane.

"And you?" I asked, refusing to let her off quite so easily. "Why are you still here? Why haven't you moved on?" I paused, waited for her to reply. But instead of answering, she bit down on her lip and quickly looked away. "I mean, I'm assuming you know about the bridge that leads to the other side, *right*?" I cocked my head to the side, which caused my hair to fall into my eyes. But the longer I waited for her to speak up, the more silence I got. "I mean, it's not like *I'm* going to take you there or anything. It's not like that's any of my business. I'm just curious. That's all."

I shoved my bangs back off my face and cast an anxious glance all around. The Council was privy to every single thing that went down, leaving me to hope they'd at least caught on to the fact that I'd finally learned my lesson. That I had no further interest in making up my own assignments, much less catching souls that weren't mine to catch. Theocoles was my one and *only* concern, the only one I'd be crossing over on this particular visit to Rome.

Still, I figured it couldn't hurt to at least *mention* the bridge. Just in case she didn't yet know about it . . . or something.

She turned, her dark eyes narrowing as she regarded me closely. Her hand caught in her hair, twirling a tendril around the very tip of her finger. She said, "I'm surprised they sent you." She continued to scrutinize me. "You appear much younger than all of the previous Soul Catchers. *Much* younger, in fact."

If she was trying to insult me, well, it didn't work. I just shrugged it right off, or at least that's the impression I struggled to give.

"The last one they sent was much older. Much bigger too, for that matter—blended right in with the rest of them. Maybe a little *too* well, come to think of it, seeing as he never did find his way out . . ." Her lip curled as she tilted her head toward the crowd of grunting, lunging gladiators. Her stream of dark curls swinging over her shoulder as she added, "He's still here. Somewhere. Every now and then I run into him. Or should I say *them*. Make no mistake, it's not like he's the only one who lost his way . . ."

She was doing her best to intimidate me, and I needed her to know right from the start that while I may look young, and scrawny, and pretty much completely incapable of dealing with any ghost, much less a gladiator ghost— for whatever unfathomable reason, the Council saw fit to assign me. Which clearly meant that despite all outward appearances, I had myself some major Soul Catching mojo working in my favor.

"I know about the others," I said, crossing my arms before me.

"Do you?" She looked me over, the words spoken so softly I could just barely hear them. Her voice gaining in pitch when she added, "Well, in that case, I'll just say that you are the very first girl that they've sent to these parts— ever. Which is something I find very interesting, don't you?"

I looked her over, screwed my mouth to the side, acting as though I found it only mildly interesting, if that.

Watching as her cheeks widened, blooming into a sudden smile as she said, "Though, who knows? It's so very odd it might actually work!" Her face radiant, beaming, but only briefly—the illusion quickly fading when she added, "Though it's really quite doubtful, to be sure."

I'd heard enough. I mean, it's not like I'd traveled all that way to win her vote. My confidence was shaky enough, the last thing I needed was some sparkly princess in a fancy red dress to grind away what little I had left.

I shook my head, narrowed my gaze, and was just about to fire off some well-worn cliché, like: *Yeah, well, don't judge a book by its cover!*

Or: *Good things come in small packages!*

Or: *You ain't seen nothing yet—prepare to be amazed!*

But before I could get there, she moved toward me. Bridging the small gap between us, she offered her hand, and said, "Still, there is only one way to know for sure."

I gulped down a mouthful of hot, dusty air and stared at her waiting, outstretched hand. All too aware that I'd just reached the part that usually, if not always, wound up dragging me headfirst into a whole heap of trouble.

And yet, that still didn't stop me from smiling as I took it in mine.

I mean, it was just like she said, *There was only one way to know for sure*, and I had to start somewhere.

5

While I'm not exactly sure what I expected to happen—I did expect *something* to happen. In the past, that sort of hand-to-hand contact always led to me finding myself trapped in some super scary world that I had to fight like heck to bust my way out of. Which is why I was a little more than surprised to find us still standing there, hands still clasped together as the girl smiled and said, "You may call me Messalina."

I nodded, continuing to brace for the big, dramatic *thing*. But when it didn't happen, when it turned out to be just your standard, everyday kind of handshake, I freed myself from her grasp and said, "I'm Riley. Riley Bloom. And while it's been really great talking to you, the thing is, I have a job to do. I really need to find a way to get through to Theocoles. So, if you have any helpful hints, any sort of insider info, I'd love to hear it. But if not . . ." I shrugged, figuring there was no need to mince words. "Well, then we should probably say our goodbyes since I really need to move this thing along."

I'd just barely finished, when she did the most unexpected thing: Instead of getting mad, or huffy, or completely offended—she laughed at me.

She stood right there before me and laughed in this gorgeous, girly way I would never be capable of no matter how hard I might try.

When I laughed, my cheeks spread too wide, my eyes went all squinty and watery, my nose turned bright red, and if it was something really funny, well, this horrible sound—a cross between a snort and a honk—would find its way out, which usually just got me going again. In short, there was nothing pretty about it.

But when Messalina laughed, it was reminiscent of wind chimes tinkling in a light summer breeze. Her shoulders lifted in a way that made her long glossy curls bounce and sway, as her cheeks flushed the color of rosebuds, and her eyes sparkled in delight.

It was almost too much.

Almost enough to make me dislike her right there on the spot.

Bringing her heavily jeweled fingers to her mouth, she finally quieted down enough to say, "Are you *always* in such a big hurry?"

I took a moment to consider, then said, "Yes. Pretty much always." Unable to see what was so funny.

But when her eyes met mine the weirdest thing happened— all the annoyance that just a moment before threatened to consume me just melted away. The feel of her gaze so comforting, it was like slipping into a warm, inviting bath.

"Well, that's too bad," she said. "That just won't do around here. Ever hear the saying: *When in Rome, do as the Romans do?*"

I shrugged, stared at my feet, not wanting to let on that I hadn't. Not wanting to look completely stupid in her eyes.

"You can't just rush in, Riley. If you want to reach Theocoles, you must first **understand** Theocoles. You have to become familiar with his world, the time that he lived in, the reason he chooses to linger in the way that he does. And, as it just so happens, I can help you with that."

She extended her hand once again, her gaze serene, her smile gentle, but unlike the last time, I didn't accept it. I just stood there and stared at the way her hand hovered before me, acting as though she had all the time in the world for me to make up my mind.

I glanced between her and Theocoles, who was kicking up a thick cloud of dust as he put himself through a series of jumps and kicks that were soon followed by crouches and rolls before he returned to the jumping and kicking again.

Totally oblivious of her, of me, of everything around him—tuned in only to the vision that played in his head—leaving me with no doubt that my options were few.

I was in foreign territory in more ways than one. So what could it hurt to take her hand once again—to accept her offer of help? It's not like I hesitated the first time around, so why was I suddenly so filled with doubt?

Because it could hurt plenty! The thought lodged itself in my head. *You could get stuck and never find your way out—just like all the Soul Catchers that were sent here before you!*

Still, as much as I knew that to be true, it wasn't enough to stop me from mashing my lips, meeting her gaze, and saying, "On one condition, and one condition only." Knowing it was a little weird for me to be the one making the ultimatum when I was dependent on her.

She nodded, her face appearing so beautiful, so kind, so trusting, so open, I almost felt bad for continuing.

Almost, but not quite.

I cleared my throat, kept my hands firmly by my sides, and added, "The condition being that you will not trap me, terrorize me, taunt me, or . . . or anything even remotely resembling that. You will help me to understand Theocoles, his world, his motivations, and whatever else I need to know so that I can get through to him and convince him that it's time to move on. And when it's time for me to leave—I leave.

I'm not like the other Soul Catchers you've met. I mean, no offense or anything, but I'm not all that fond of this place. I've yet to see one good reason to stay. Which means I *will* find my way back. There's no way you can keep me here any longer than I want. No matter how hard you try."

She paused. Her bottom lip pushed into a ridiculously pretty pout, her expression rearranging itself into one of deep contemplation as her brown eyes met mine and she said, "And what makes you think that *I'm* responsible for the fate of those previous Soul Catchers?"

I narrowed my gaze, not missing a beat when I answered, "My gut." I kept my voice stern, businesslike, wanting her to know I'd meant what I'd said. "My gut tells me you're not all that you seem. And, just so you know, my gut is rarely, if ever, wrong about these things."

She ducked her head, allowing a bird's eye view of the beautiful ruby pinned in her hair. Then lifting it again, she smiled as though she really did mean it when she said, "You have a deal, Miss Riley Bloom." Her eyes glittered with excitement. "So, what do you say? Are you ready to travel even deeper into Theocoles' world?"

She thrust her hand before me, palm open, fingers beckoning, and just like the first time, I didn't hesitate. I just gritted my teeth, closed my eyes, and once again, took her hand in mine.

6

The second before I opened my eyes, I cringed. My jaw clenched, my shoulders pulled in, my entire being on high alert, bracing for the scene I was sure I would find myself in: me, cowering inside the Colosseum, caught smack dab in the middle of some grisly, blood-soaked battle fought to the death—one that involved pitchforks, swords, horse-driven chariots, and, just my luck, a gang of ferocious, ravenous lions.

So imagine my surprise when instead of finding myself immersed in some gruesome scene of slaughter, surrounded by a cheering, bloodthirsty crowd, I found myself standing in the most luxurious dressing room I've ever seen.

"Wow," I murmured, not wanting to appear overly impressed, but still, I couldn't keep the word from sneaking out. I'd never seen anything even remotely like it, except for maybe on movies or TV, but never in real life, and certainly never in the afterlife. "Where are we?" I turned toward Messalina, wondering why she saw fit to bring me here—not that I was complaining, but still, it didn't seem to make any sense.

Messalina laughed—that lovely, tinkling sound bouncing off the elaborately carved marble columns and walls, echoing all around. "This is my home," she told me, clearly amused by my reaction.

"You *live* here?" My eyes grew wide as I strained to take it all in—the chaise longue strewn with colorful silk throws and piles of elaborately embroidered pillows—the jumble of combs and jewels and scented oils and crèmes that littered a nearby table—the shiny, sparkly heaps of what could only be described as "girly-type-things" that draped over every available surface and spilled out of an assortment of ornately painted trunks.

"And is that—is that an *indoor* swimming pool?" I gestured toward a shallow, mosaic tiled pool, off in its own separate room—the water strewn with lovely pink rose petals that floated along the top, as the flickering torches glittered brightly against the white marble walls.

I couldn't keep from gaping. Couldn't keep from wondering why I'd never thought to manifest something like that for myself. Vowing to remedy that as soon as I returned to my home in the Here & Now.

"This is my room, and that is my bath." Messalina cracked a slow, careful smile. "Though I wouldn't exactly say that I *live* here. This is the place where I was raised, Riley. It is also where I met my death, many, many, *many* years ago."

My gaze strayed from her to her things; there was so much to look at, it was hard to take it all in. "Well, I guess I can see why you stay." I shrugged. "Unlike those gladiators down in the barracks, this is a pretty chichi place you got yourself here."

"It is nice, and comfortable, to be sure." She shot me a stern look as she added, "But make no mistake—it is *not* why I stay. Not even close."

I turned toward her, my attention claimed by the unmistakable edge in her voice. "So why do you stay?" I asked, knowing it was time to get down to business. Time to be a little less impressed by my luxurious surroundings, and a little more focused on the reason I'd taken her hand and followed her here.

But Messalina had her own agenda, and instead of answering, she just shot me another stern look and said, "Still trying to rush this along, are you?" She shook her head, brought her hand to her temple where she sought to tame a renegade curl by tucking it back behind her ear. "You will learn everything, Riley, all in good time, I give you my word. But first, if you want to learn about Theocoles' world, you will have to make some adjustments to fit into that world."

"What's that supposed to mean?" My voice pitched high with suspicion, watching as she pressed a long, delicate finger to the tip of her chin as her eyes narrowed in study—rapidly traveling the length of me, up and down, back and forth, over and over again, stopping only when she'd reached some sort of conclusion.

"Well, for starters, we must do something about your clothes." She wagged her finger at my outfit as though she found it both sad and offensive. "I'm sorry to have to say it, but this sort of attire just will not do."

I was outraged. Stunned speechless. I mean, seriously, if she found my outfit offensive, that was nothing compared to the offense I took to the sneer she wore on her face.

"Uh, for your information," I said, doing my best to keep my voice steady and my emotions in check, despite how annoyed I was getting. "*This*—" I jabbed my thumb toward the center of my chest. "This just so happens to be all the rage back on the earth plane. I'll have you know that Miley Cyrus wore this exact same T-shirt when she stepped out for a latte and the paparazzi stalked her with a supersized telephoto lens just so they could get a really clear picture of her. And while I get that you've been dead for like a gazillion years, and probably don't even know who Miley Cyrus is, let me just state that, for the record—"

"Riley, please—" She cut in, her hand raised, her palm flashing between us. "I know who Miley Cyrus is. I can move quite easily between ancient Rome and modern Rome, you know. Though admittedly, I do choose to spend most of my time here. And while I'm sorry to have offended you, I only meant to suggest that your modern clothing has no place in this world. If you want to blend in then you'll have to first dress the part. And later, you'll have to learn to play the part as well."

"So, what then?" I asked, unwilling to give in so easily. I liked my look, my clothes were brand new, recently manifested, and in order to change them, I was going to need a little more convincing than she'd given so far. "You going to put me in some filthy gladiator tunic in hopes that I'll somehow find a way to miraculously blend in among all those vicious killers? 'Cause, sorry for saying so, but I highly doubt that'll work. I highly doubt I'll fit in."

I shook my head, started to mumble a few additional words not really meant for her ears, but didn't get very far before I was surprised into silence when she placed her hands on her hips, leaned toward me, and said, "First of all—they're not *all* vicious killers." She paused, allowing enough time for her words to sink in and take root, her eyes glinting when she added, "I can see how on the surface you might think that—but if you want to complete your mission here, then you must never group them so carelessly together. You must never forget that there's much more to their story than that which you've witnessed so far. Each and every one of them has their own unique reason for doing what they do. I think you'll be very surprised to learn what they are. And second—you have a very difficult time trusting people, don't you?" She looked me over, her gaze clearly saddened by the thought, though I was quick to correct her.

"No, not people. Just ghosts," I snapped, mimicking her body language by placing my own hands on my hips and leaning toward her until our noses nearly touched. "And believe me, I've got my reasons. I've been burned more than once. And I don't plan to ever let that happen again."

I nodded to confirm it, making it clear that I was not one to be messed with, but Messalina turned away. Busying herself with a trunk full of shiny, silky, beautiful things she began sorting through.

"Well then, allow me to say that it is my sincerest wish that you will learn to relax and trust me." She flashed me a smile from over her shoulder. "I truly hope that we can be friends. It's been such a long time since I've enjoyed the companionship of a girl my own age."

I shoved my hands deep into my front pockets and shot her a quizzical look. It'd been a while since I'd had a friend too, and it was something I was really starting to miss, but surely she didn't think we were the same age? Surely she realized there were a handful of birthdays between us?

"But, until then," she continued, deflecting my look with a wave of her hand. "What do you say we exchange your blue jeans and Miley Cyrus tee for *this*?"

My gaze shifted, and I watched in wonder as she pulled a stream of soft, silky, blue fabric from the trunk and dangled it from the tips of her fingers—the flame from the torches, along with the soft slant of light that spilled in from the windows, bathing it in the most astonishing, incandescent glow that left it shimmering before me.

It was my all-time favorite shade of blue—a deep and vibrant aquamarine. A color that instantly conjured up images of lazy days spent floating on a beautiful tropical sea. Not that I'd ever spent a lazy day like that, but still, that's exactly what it made me think of. And as I watched her move toward me, the fabric swishing and rippling between us, I knew I couldn't, wouldn't resist. It was far too tempting to miss.

She pressed the fabric to my front and fussed a bit with the shoulders and waist, her lips pressed tightly together as she yanked and tugged and tried to gauge the fit.

"What do you think?" she asked, as I peered down at myself. "Do you like it? I think it really brings out the blue of your eyes."

"It really is beautiful," I admitted. Though I also had to admit to myself that it would look a lot less beautiful once I was actually wearing it. Now that she held it against me, there was no denying it just wouldn't work.

I mean, don't get me wrong, I'm really into clothes and stuff, and I like to think I've got pretty good taste despite what Messalina might think. But the kind of stuff I wear is usually a bit sportier than the dress she was foisting on me—a dress that was long, and flowy, and formal, and really kind of important looking.

The kind of dress you might wear if you were ever nominated for an Oscar, or a Grammy, or something.

The kind of dress that required a body that could actually fill up the fabric—the kind of body I'd long been denied.

Seriously, all you had to do was take one quick look to know that we were both headed for a major disappointment. The second I slipped on that dress it would cease to ripple and flow in that magical way. Instead it would sag and droop like an overcooked noodle.

"Um, do you have something else?" I pushed it away as though I found it offensive. "Something a little better suited to . . . well . . . someone like me?"

Messalina looked me over, her head cocked, brows drawn together. "*This* is suited for someone like you. Some-one *exactly* like you, to be sure. C'mon, Riley, why not take a chance and try it on? I think you'll find yourself quite surprised by the result."

Her eyes coaxed, her voice bordered on insistent, but as tempting as it was to take her word for it, I knew better.

I just wasn't up for that kind of humiliation.

I just wasn't up for confirming what I already knew.

But despite my protest, Messalina remained persistent—she would not give in easily. "Don't forget, you've left your world far behind. You're in my world now. So please, why don't you just try to trust me? Why don't you just take a chance, try on the dress, and see for yourself?"

While I had no idea why it was so dang important to her, I did know there was no use in fighting her. From what I could tell, we were equally matched in the stubborn department, which meant the longer I fought, the longer it would take me to get down to business, finish the job, and get the heck out—something I desperately wanted to do.

I heaved a loud sigh—leaving no doubt as to just how reluctant I was to cooperate—then I surrendered to the dress, allowing her to slip that filmy, blue fabric right over my head.

Her fingers moved deftly, quickly, as she tucked, and draped, and tied, and pinched, and pulled, and fussed—all the while making soft, little clucking sounds as her tongue repeatedly hit the roof of her mouth. And even though I was tempted to peek, she'd given strict orders that I was to either close my eyes, or stare straight ahead. I wasn't allowed to look at the final result, until she gave the OK.

The moment the dress was in place, she started messing with the rest of me as well. Twisting and pulling at my hair, pinning it in place with all manner of shiny jeweled ornaments she'd plucked from the table beside her. Then, after attaching some earrings to my ears, and clasping a heavy, jeweled necklace behind my neck, she told me to close my eyes—well, it was actually more like a demand—and since I was already in the mode of obeying, I did.

"And keep 'em closed," she said, as soon as I'd done as she asked. "No peeking until I say when. Promise?" I sighed in reply, fully convinced she was setting me up for what would only amount to a major fail on both our parts.

Her feet padding softly against the floor as she moved to wrestle with something in a corner—her sudden return announced by the hum of her murmuring voice at my ear, saying, "Now, I want you to think very hard. I want you to concentrate *not* on the image you're convinced that you'll see, but rather on the one you *desire* to see."

"You mean, like ... *manifesing*?" My entire being drooped in frustration, sure it would never work.

While I was well used to manifesting—well used to imagining whatever it is that I wanted—things like clothes,

and books, and iPods, and new furniture for my room—
and then seeing it appear right before me like the magic it
was—I knew for a fact that it would never work on myself.
I mean, it's not like I hadn't already thought of that—it's not
like I hadn't already tried.

But, for whatever reason, Messalina was convinced, and
she was more than determined to convince me as well. "Yes,
it's exactly like manifesting," she said. "And in order for it to
work, I need you to clear your mind of any lingering doubt.
Remember, Riley, you're in my world now."

To be honest, I felt a little silly standing there with my
body swallowed whole by that baggy blue dress, and my
eyes all squinched shut as I tried to envision a version of me
that would never, ever be.

And yet, part of me figured, *what the heck*? It's not like
I had much to lose. I mean, hadn't Bodhi told me that if I
wanted to be a teen then I had to see myself as a teen? That
I had to learn how to act as if I already had it? If it worked,
well, then I'd finally realize my dream—and the thought of
that alone made it well worth the risk of looking any dumber
than I already did.

I squeezed my lids tighter, tempted to really dive in,
go all out, and imagine myself looking like a movie star,
a supermodel, or maybe even a hybrid of both. But before
the image could begin to take shape, I quickly erased it and

started again. Figuring it would be far more interesting to see a version of me that truly lived up to my full (and far more probable) potential, as opposed to an image my own mom wouldn't recognize.

"Can you see her?" Messalina's voice was tinged with excitement. "Can you see the new you blossom like a flower in your mind?"

She brushed a cool finger across my brow as I continued to concentrate as hard as I could. Focusing on a version of me that wasn't so entirely different from how I actually was—only better—taller. One where the baby fat that once padded my face had made way for a nice pair of cheekbones that somehow, miraculously, made my semi-stubby nose appear . . . well . . . not quite so semi-stubby.

Oh, and of course I gave myself hair that was thicker, and wavier, and a whole lot glossier too—the kind of hair you see in shampoo ads. And when it came time for imaginings below the neck, well, let's just say that I was quick to transform my stick figure into one with just the right amount of swoops and curves that would serve the dress well.

With the image firmly fixed in my mind, I gave a quick nod so Messalina would know it was done. And when she clapped her hands together and said, "Look!"—I did.

Gazing into the full-length mirror she'd propped up before me, I gasped in delight at a vision of me that looked a lot like my beautiful, older sister Ever, while also managing to stay true to me—albeit, a much better, prettier, more mature version of me.

I looked exactly like the image I'd conjured in my head.

"So, what do you think? Do you like what you see? I was right about the dress, wasn't I?" Messalina's voice was as anxious as the expression she wore on her face.

My fingers grazed first over the mirror, and then over myself—hardly able to grasp the enormous change that had just taken place. My face broke into a smile as I glanced her way, my eyes shiny, my cheeks beaming, my voice gone hoarse but still bearing the full extent of my gratitude when I said, "Oh yes, I like it very much. I look at least . . ." I turned back toward my image, scrutinized it closely. Starting to say: *I look thirteen—the age I've always wanted to be!*—but soon realizing I'd managed to pass thirteen right by.

Maybe even fourteen as well.

And quite possibly fifteen too.

"How old are *you*?" I asked, looking her over again, hoping to gauge my own progress against hers, since she still appeared older than me.

But Messalina just shrugged. Her shoulders rising and falling in that graceful, delicate way that she had. "I don't know," she said. "I guess no one ever thought to keep track."

My eyes bugged in a way that wasn't one bit pretty, but

I couldn't help it. I'd never heard of such a thing. It was so outrageous, so unthinkable, I immediately suspected her of lying.

"My parents died when I was quite young," she continued, her voice steady, the words matter of fact, with no hint of the emotion she might've felt at that long-ago time. "I lived with a series of reluctant relatives until I landed here. The *ludus* belonged to my uncle, my aunt was unable to conceive and found herself so desperate for a child, she settled for me. And while I've spent many years in this place, I can't say exactly how many. All I know is I was a child when I arrived, and when I died, I looked like this." She ran a hand down her side.

"So you never had a birthday party?" I tried my best to quash my surprise, but still, it really was unthinkable, an outrage for sure. I couldn't even imagine such a thing. Birthdays had always been extremely important to me.

She squinted, tilted her head to the side, acting as though my reaction was completely unfathomable, as though she couldn't understand why I'd place such importance on something that to her was just as easily forgotten, if not ignored.

Her reaction prompting me to wave it away, end it right there. We were products of different times, different cultures—there was no point in getting sidetracked by things that couldn't possibly help me with the job I came to do.

Returning to my own, glorious transformation, the newly grown-up version of me, I moved closer to the mirror, ran a hand over my shiny, springy curls that cascaded all the way down to my waist, taking in the pale green shimmer that glowed all around me—remembering how it used to glow a little bit darker, a little bit deeper, until things didn't go so well on my last unassigned Soul Catch and all of my progress faded away. Pretty much the opposite of Bodhi's glow, which continued to shine brighter—the green edged out by blue until it became a beautiful, vibrant aqua—the same shade as the dress I was wearing.

My guide had left me in the dust. Effortlessly moving onto fifteen while I was stuck at twelve. And yet, if he could see how quickly I'd just progressed, I was sure he'd be as awestruck as I was. The only thing that marred the transformation was that stupid, barely there glimmer of mine.

"Is everything okay?" Messalina peered at me, her face clouded with concern. "Are you not happy with the new you?"

I glanced between our reflections, unable to see my dismal green glow as anything other than what it truly was—a constant reminder of what I'd done wrong. A painful memory of what I'd already learned. And it's not like lugging it around was doing me the least bit of good.

Messalina didn't glow. Neither did any of the other ghosts I'd seen around the *ludus*. And if the goal was for me to find a way to fit in as best as I could, well, then it was clear that my glow-on needed to *move on*.

I lowered my lids, imagining the way I'd look without that annoying, greenish-tinged glow—and when I lifted them again, it was gone. Easy-peasy—simple as that. Leaving me with a perfected version of the newly improved, glorious me.

Messalina stared, her eyes bright and anxious, playing at the rings she wore on her hands, eager for me to react in some way, let her know how I felt about my sudden transformation, and I was quick to relieve her.

"This is everything I've dreamed of for so long!" I ran my hands over my dress as my face curved into a grin. "I feel like a butterfly that just burst free of its cocoon." My eyes met hers, wondering if there was any way to express the full depth of my gratitude. "I truly have no idea how I'll ever go about thanking you," I said, meaning every last word.

Messalina smiled and reached toward me. Capturing my hand between hers, she led me away from the room. "No need to worry about that right now," she said. "We'll have plenty of time for that later, to be sure. But for now, just a few final touches." She stopped before a beautiful tray where she scooped up a pile of glimmering, golden rings, taking careful consideration of the offerings before selecting two she then handed to me. "They're exact replicas of the ones I wear." She smiled, holding her hand up and wiggling her fingers for me to see. "I hope you'll consider this as a seal of our friendship." She watched as I slipped the rings onto my fingers, her grin growing wider when the task was complete. "Actually, we are closer than friends now, we are more like sisters, wouldn't you agree?"

I frowned, all too ready to disagree. Being friends was one thing, pretending to be sisters was another thing entirely. I already had a sister—one who I loved, and admired, and greatly missed—one who could never, ever be replaced.

I was just about to tell Messalina as much, when she ran a light finger across the width of my forehead and the strangest sensation swept over me. A swarm of kindness, and acceptance that made all of my former loneliness disappear, until I couldn't help but think: *What the heck? What could it hurt to pretend?*

And the next thing I knew, I was smiling and giggling, ready to follow wherever she led. Crooking my arm around hers as she said, "So now, sister, we must hurry—we have ourselves a very glamorous party to attend!"

7

I know it sounds vain. I know it sounds completely self-centered and more than a little obnoxious—but I couldn't help it—I just couldn't stop staring at myself.

Every reflective surface I passed became another opportunity for me to gawk, and gape, and marvel, and basically just outright ogle my shiny, new self.

It was the makeover to end all makeovers, and I just couldn't get enough of it.

"You are quite beautiful, I assure you," Messalina whispered, her voice far more amused than annoyed, her hand pressed firmly to the small of my back as she guided me down the length of a very large room. "This must be rather exciting for you, no?"

A servant strolled by balancing a long silver platter that my eyes eagerly chased. Dismissing the tall pile of fruit that sprawled along its top, I went straight for the edges, my gaze drawn to the place where my image beamed back, broken and distorted for sure—but still far more pleasing to look at than ever before.

"So, where are we?" I asked, as soon as the servant moved on. It was time to get over myself and focus on the business at hand. But with all the surrounding excitement and splendor, it was getting harder and harder to do.

There was so much flamboyance, so much opulence and wealth, so much sparkly glitz and glamour—my head practically spun on my neck in an effort to take it all in.

Every surface gleamed. Every table sagged under mountains of sweets and treats and towering heaps of delicacies that a parade of servants constantly replenished. The room dotted with petal-strewn fountains, the floors covered by intricate mosaic designs, and yet despite the glorious décor, it was the other partygoers who really stole my attention.

The females all dripping with the finest array of satins and silks, sporting bright, shiny jewels the size of small fists—and the males were no different, dressed in elaborate tunics with glittering braided bits that swooped around the necklines and hems, while thick golden chains swung from their necks.

It was the kind of life one could easily get used to—easily get lost in. After just a short time there, I could already see why some of those other Soul Catchers had chosen to stay.

It was the opposite of the world I first stumbled upon—as different from the *ludus* as you could possibly get.

"The games begin tomorrow." Messalina's gaze moved among the assorted guests before finding her way back to me. "And though the games themselves are considered to be the best part of the celebration, think of this as a sort of . . . kickoff party." She smiled in a way that didn't quite reach her eyes. "A party intended to commemorate the start of the games."

The games, right. Gladiators. Theocoles. The real reason you're here. Stay focused, Riley—sheesh!

"So the party is for the games?" I asked, knowing it was redundant, but determined to get back on track.

"Indeed." She nodded. "These games are in honor of the emperor's death. They are funeral games, as most games are. Meant to honor powerful men whose time has come, and the longer the games run, the more important the man—or so it is thought. And believe me, these particular games are meant to provide the biggest, splashiest spectacle yet. No expense has been spared, as you will soon see." She gazed around the room again, as though searching for someone, her gaze far away when she said, "Hundreds of gladiators are scheduled to compete, and thousands of wild beasts have been brought from as far away as Africa just to take part."

I struggled to imagine such an endeavor. Having to

remind myself that I was caught in a time that existed long before cars, planes, trams, or trains, all of which made such a journey seem completely incomprehensible.

"They traveled on a series of boats and rafts and then were loaded onto horse-drawn caravans, just so they could die a spectacular death before bloodthirsty crowds that demanded nothing less." She sighed and shook her head, her glorious curls swinging back and forth. "Which is not so different from the way the gladiators will die, some of whom made the trip alongside them."

"It sounds awful," I said, my voice turned suddenly serious, my mood suddenly sobered, no longer drunk on my shiny new self.

"It is, to be sure." She nodded. "Though, I must confess I was once no better than the rest of them." She gestured toward the glittering crowd. "*Panem et circenses.*" She pronounced the words easily, with a beautiful lilt I never could've managed. "Which translates to **bread and circus**. The bread being that which they throw to the crowd during the course of the games in order to keep them fed throughout a long day, and the circus being the games themselves. 'Keep the lower classes appeased by bread and circus, and they will be yours'—or so it was said. But make no mistake, the upper classes were just as enthralled. I once considered the games and all of those horrible deaths as the highest form of amusement. But then, one day, one of those deaths touched me personally, and from that moment on, everything changed . . ."

I stayed silent, clinging fast to her words. Realizing she'd just revealed something deeply personal, and wondering if the hint was intentional. Everything about her seemed calculated—there was nothing careless about her.

Was she referring to Theocoles? I'd seen the way she'd gazed down at him from her perch on the balcony. Clearly she'd known him, but how? Had they been close? The idea of it seemed impossible. They were from two different worlds—two different worlds that sometimes overlapped, but still.

"Weren't all of the gladiators slaves?" I asked, trying to keep my tone casual, figuring she'd cut me off the second she sensed I was prying. She had an agenda—of that I was sure—one she controlled as tightly as she controlled her own world.

"Yes," she said. "Though while it is true that the majority of them were slaves, make no mistake—they were among the strongest, bravest, most fierce of all. My uncle had an eye for these things. Other *ludus* owners watched him quite closely in the slave markets, trying their best to outbid him, but they rarely succeeded. My uncle had very deep pockets, along with a sort of second sight—a gift for these things—if you could call that a gift." She waved a dismissive hand, causing the sparkling ring on her finger to catch and reflect the torchlight. "Though, that's not to say that they all began as slaves. I know it may seem strange to you, but there were also those who volunteered, those who signed a contract with my uncle—eagerly exchanging their time and talents for the possibility of winnings and glory. Being a gladiator held its own unique brand of honor—they were both respected and feared. You must realize, Riley, that the Colosseum easily housed up to fifty thousand people, and more often than not, it was filled to capacity. I guess you could say they were like the rock stars of their time—they ruled the arena like gods. Boys who hailed from soft lives and nobility mimicked their moves, while countless women swooned over them—their affections displayed in the small, blood-dipped swords they'd pin in their hair."

She slewed her eyes to the side, her face taking on an expression I couldn't quite read, and despite hearing everything she'd just said, there was one part in particular that I couldn't quite grasp.

"So you're serious—people actually *volunteered* to fight in the arena, and risk a grisly, violent death?" My eyes grew wide. I couldn't imagine such a thing. From what little I knew, the arena had been a savage and brutally terrifying place.

"There were many reasons for that," Messalina snapped, her voice adopting an annoyed, impatient tone. "Some more complicated than others, I might add." I was just about to gently prod her for more, when she waved her hand before her, smiled sweetly, and said, "So, tell me, what do you think of the party?"

I glanced around the room, not quite sure how to answer. Suddenly feeling shamed by my initial reaction of awe, the thrill of being part of it all, and no longer able to view my surroundings in quite the same way as before.

All of those bright, shiny people who seemed so glamorous just a few moments ago, now appeared savage and depraved, immoral and bloodthirsty in the very worst way. All of those servants bearing the heaping platters of food were not there by choice—they were just as enslaved as the gladiators. Slaves to the house instead of the arena, but still slaves all the same.

"Are all of these people ghosts?" I asked, directing the conversation to a more neutral subject, partly because I was reluctant to annoy her again, and partly because I really was curious. "Are all of these people choosing to haunt this place?"

I gave the room another once-over, wondering why so many slaves would choose to linger in such a wretched, thankless role. But then, it was just like she'd already told me—every ghost had a story. And while I hoped someday they'd find a way to move on, that wasn't my job. I was there to learn about Theocoles, to focus on the lost soul that had been assigned to me, and no more.

"Some are ghosts, some are not." Messalina shrugged. "My intention was to recreate the celebration exactly as I remember it, so that you can better understand the world that Theocoles lives in."

"So, where is he?" I glanced around the room without really expecting to find him. After all, Theocoles was a slave, a gladiator; I seriously doubted he had any real part in this world—or at least not this side of it—the more glamorous side of it. "Is he here? Was he allowed to come to parties like this?"

Messalina nodded, her face cautious, guarded, her arm rising, finger pointing, as she said, "He is right over there."

I followed the gesture to where a group of gladiators stood at attention, their arms and legs shackled, as a crowd of partygoers stopped to inspect them. Pushing and prodding as though the fierce warriors displayed before them existed for no other reason than to quench the crowd's morbid amusement.

I started to rush toward him, but didn't get very far before I was stopped by the firm grasp of Messalina's long cool fingers encircling my wrist. "Not now." She looked at me, her smile tight, forced, not the least bit genuine. "You will meet him soon enough, I give you my word. But for now, we have much more pressing matters to attend to. We must find a new name with which to call you."

I looked her over, my face dropping into a frown, not liking the sound of that, not liking it at all. I mean, how could that possibly be more important than my meeting Theocoles? And besides, wasn't it enough that I'd changed my appearance? Now she had to mess with my name as well?

But before I could lodge a complaint, a slave bearing a large clay jug brushed up against me, bumping me in a way that set me so off balance, got me so spun around, I found myself facing the opposite side of the room where I saw something so incredibly startling, all I could do was freeze right there in place.

Only this time it wasn't a shiny, reflective surface that distracted me.

This time it was a boy.

A boy who looked at me in a way that . . . well, in a way that I'd never been looked at before.

With curiosity.

And intensity.

Along with a healthy dose of unmistakable interest.

The same way boys used to look at my sister, Ever—the way they looked at Messalina—but never, not once, at me.

Or at least not the old version of me.

My face grew hot while my hands went all shaky, and I continued to stand there all frozen and stupid and utterly foolish.

I had no idea what to do. No idea how to react. I was as clueless to the customs of the time as I was to being stared at by boys.

I continued like that, a frozen, gaping mess, until Messalina finally stepped in and saved me from my own awkward self, when she said, "It's like I said earlier, you not only need to *look* the part—you also need to *play* the part. C'mon, it'll be fun." She reached toward my forehead, smiling as she ran a finger across the width of my brow, pushing a loose curl to the side—the feel of her touch stealing my anxiety and leaving calm in its place. "I've done the hard work for you—I've narrowed it down to two choices, either of which will do, either of which will suit you. So go ahead, you choose— which name do you prefer: Lauricia or Aurelia?" Her eyes flashed as brightly as the jewels that swung from her ears. "Hurry! We must decide quickly," she whispered, nodding toward the opposite side of the room, her voice brisk and impatient, when she added, "In case you haven't yet noticed, you've managed to cause quite a bit of a stir with one guest in particular. And from what I can tell it's just a matter of time before he'll be standing before us, demanding to know who you are, and we'll need something to tell him, now won't we?"

I paused for a moment, acting as though I was giving serious consideration to each name, when the truth is I'd already chosen Aurelia. I'd claimed it the moment I heard it. If for no other reason than it reminded me of Aurora—the most beautiful, serene, accomplished member of the Council, who, as it just so happened, was also my favorite. And yet, it also contained a hint of my own name as well, which pretty much made it the perfect combination.

But before I had a chance to inform Messalina, the boy from across the room was already standing before us. His gaze darting between Messalina and me, as he said, "Messalina, always a pleasure." He ducked his head low, taking her hand in his so that he could bring his lips to it. Then nodding toward me he added, "And who is this you've brought with you?" His gaze locked on mine.

Messalina shot me an anxious look—unsure what to call me. Though it's not like it mattered. At that moment, it was like time was suspended.

As though the entire party was set on pause.

As though nothing else existed but his dark tousled hair, smooth olive skin, and deeply brown, almost black eyes that made my head swirl.

"My name is Aurelia," I said, my voice surprisingly sure,

extending my hand with a strange rush of calm.

I had no idea where it came from. No idea how I'd found myself slipping so easily into the role of a young and sophisticated Roman aristocrat. And yet, there I was—my gaze lowered shyly, my lips curving flirtatiously, a puff of air rounding my cheeks, as I waited to feel the brush of his palm, the brief sweep of his lips on my hand—the standard greeting of the time. It was as though I really was Aurelia, and at that moment, I preferred her to me.

"Aurelia, this is Dacian," Messalina informed me, her eyes flashing knowingly. "As you well know, Dacian is the son of a senator," she added, carefully stating her words, clearly wanting me to get the significance. Dacian was important, someone I should at least pretend to know.

"Strange we have not met before," Dacian said, his voice as perplexed as his face, as though he truly was struggling to make sense of it.

I shrugged, my shoulders rising and falling as I cast my gaze to the side, amazed by the amount of cool I displayed, though it wasn't long before it began ebbing away and I was cast out of the role Messalina insisted I play.

I wasn't used to being around boys that cute—and Dacian definitely fell into the category of Seriously Cute. I mean, I'd known him for less than a minute and he'd already claimed the top spot on my "Top 5 Cutest Boys Ever" list—the one that included living people, ghosts, and celebrities (and this despite the fact that his outfit pretty much resembled a dress).

Aurelia shined at that sort of thing, Riley didn't. But as much as I wanted to be Aurelia again, she was drowned out by the warning that blared in my head, an annoyingly cautious voice shouting: *Do not get distracted! Your name is not Aurelia, and Dacian is not on your agenda, no matter how cute he may be. You are here to find Theocoles and cross him over—that's it!*

The voice was loud—a lot louder than I wanted it to be. And yet, it didn't stand a chance against Messalina's when she clasped my hand in hers, instantly silencing my thoughts when she said, "Forgive me, Aurelia, but I must attend to my aunt for a moment. I trust you'll be fine in Dacian's care? I think I'm quite fit to vouch for his good and noble character." Then turning to Dacian, her voice light and flirtatious, she added, "And I trust *you* will not make me regret the praise I just heaped upon you? I trust you will be on your best behavior and act like the perfect gentleman I know you to be—at least while you're in the company of Aurelia?"

I turned toward her, my eyes begging her to stay. My suddenly coy, calm demeanor giving way to a full-blown panic at the thought of being alone with him. I may have looked older than my years, but that was just surface. Inside

I was still me. I was still skinny, scrawny, quaking in my shoes, little Riley Bloom. There was no getting around it—I was in over my head.

But if Messalina saw my pleading look, she chose to ignore it. And all I could do was watch in horror as she spun on her heel and made for the other side of the room, heading toward the space where, just a moment before, Theocoles stood.

I mumbled some flimsy excuse—moved to follow her—but I was too slow, and she was too fast, and in the end it was all I could do to keep an eye on her whereabouts.

My gaze anxiously trailing the swishy red hem of her dress, her stream of dark hair—keeping close tabs, carefully retracing each and every step, until Dacian caught up, grasped my arm lightly, and said, "Please don't leave—not when we've only just met, and I have so much still to learn about you! Where is it you come from? Why is it I've never seen or heard of you?"

My gaze only shifted for a second—less than a second, I swear—but that's all it took for me to lose sight of her. In what little time it took for me to switch my gaze from Dacian's smiling face to the space Messalina had just occupied, she was gone. And there was no doubt in my mind that she'd ditched me on purpose.

8

Dacian stared at me, waiting for a reply, but instead of answering, I ran. Leaving him to stand there, gazing after my shiny, blue dress as I sped across the room, retracing the steps Messalina had taken until I reached the spot where she'd vanished from sight.

I surveyed the area, hands on my hips, head swiveling from side to side. Seeking out all the possible routes she could've taken, while replaying her words in my mind.

She'd said she'd gone to check in with her aunt, but I immediately disregarded that, it just didn't ring true. This had something to do with Theocoles, of that I was sure.

Though I had no idea where to find him, no idea which way to go when the options were endless. Every opening of every room seemed to feed off into another, and another, and yet another, until Messalina's world began to resemble a complex labyrinth. A complex labyrinth intended to trick me, confuse me, as I'm sure it did all the other Soul Catchers before me.

Dacian called out my name, my new name, his voice cutting through the peals of laughter and party noise, as he worked his way through the crowd in hot pursuit of me. Face stricken, gaze anxious, worried he'd somehow offended me.

With only seconds to spare before he caught up, I shut my eyes tightly and forced everything into silence except my own inner voice, aware of it prodding: *The stairs—find the stairs that lead down!* Words no louder than a whisper, yet powerful all the same.

But before I could make a move, Dacian was standing before me. His voice as relieved as his face when he said, "There you are, Aurelia!" He bowed low, allowing a glimpse of his tousled brown hair, before he faced me again and his dark eyes landed on mine. "I hope I have not offended you in some way?" His face breaking into a hopeful grin made even more irresistible by the dimples that sprang up at either side of his cheeks.

And at that moment, he was so unbelievably cute I couldn't come up with one good reason to leave. Suddenly, for the first time in a long time, everything I'd ever wanted was well within reach.

I was a teen.

A beautiful teen just like my sister.

And also like my sister, cute boys were now making their way across rooms—willing to look like fools just to be near me.

I was the star of my very own fairy tale.

It was too good to resist.

So I didn't.

"Please, not to worry—it is nothing like that," I assured him, my gaze shyly meeting his. "It is only that I . . ." I knotted my brow, unsure of what followed. My voice sounded odd, containing a strange sort of lilt I didn't normally posses, never mind the words I'd just used.

Dacian crinkled his brow, took another step forward until he was standing so close I could easily make out each individual golden fleck in his dreamy brown eyes. The sight of his nearness causing me to chew my lower lip, my fingers grasping the folds of my skirt, twisting and turning the fabric until it became crumpled-up bunches I held in my fists. Vaguely aware of the voice in my head that continued to prod me toward . . . *something,* I was no longer sure what it could be.

The only thing I knew for certain was that Dacian stood before me, his grin sweet and open—his gaze charmingly hopeful—the rest was a blur.

He blinked, smiled, waited for me to finish the thought,

so I cleared my throat and dove in, trusting the right words would find their way out. My voice lighter, girlier, miles away from my usual rasp, sounding just like Aurelia's when I said, "It is only that I . . ." Dacian nodded, urging me to finish. "Well . . ." I pressed my jeweled fingers to my lips, holding back a giggle that didn't quite feel like mine. "Even though I'm a bit embarrassed to admit it, I must confess that I'm not really accustomed to . . ." *boys looking at me, flirting with me, talking to me* . . .my mind spun with the long list of possibilities. "Well, the truth is, I'm not really accustomed to these sorts of *parties*," I stammered, feeling a rush of heat rise to my cheeks, knowing that while it barely covered my long list of things I'd yet to experience, that didn't make it any less true.

Dacian leaned toward me, brow rising in surprise. "You mean to say this is your first time at the games, then?"

I nodded, trying not to squirm under his scrutiny while I twisted the rings on my fingers, hoping he would find my confession to be far more charming than pathetic.

"You did see the gladiators, though? Before they headed back down the stairs to the *ludus*?"

The stairs.

The words nudged at me, prodded me. As simple as they seemed on the surface, I couldn't help but feel that they somehow went deeper, held significant meaning.

"I hope that at the very least you were able to view the champion, Theocoles, the one they call the Pillar of Doom? Although he's considered to be favored by the gods, one must never forget that they all fall eventually. Who knows, this may have been your last chance to view him. Though I suppose tomorrow, we'll know for sure."

Theocoles.

The Pillar of Doom.

The words set off alarms in my head. Like the sound of hands clapping, fingers snapping, it was as though I'd been awakened from a very deep sleep.

Or, more like a trance.

Suddenly the magnitude of what had just happened became all too clear.

Suddenly I was all too aware of what'd happened to all of those poor Soul Catchers before me.

Messalina's world was tempting, alluring, offering the immediate promise of everything one could ever long for that seemed just out of reach. She'd enchanted me, just like she had them. She'd given me the life I'd always dreamed of—and in turn distracted me from my own plans.

Despite Bodhi's warning, despite knowing the risks, as it turns out, I was no different from the rest of my fellow Soul Catchers. I'd barely arrived, and I'd already caved.

If I had any hope of saving Theocoles—not to mention

saving myself—then I had to be more careful, more vigilant. I had to be on my guard where Messalina was concerned. I could not afford to let her enchant me again.

I had to do whatever it took to get the job done, and get the heck out. Otherwise, I'd remain stuck forever as Aurelia—a girl so different from me, I'd never be found.

Dacian may hold the number one spot on my "Cute" list, but I was there to do a job—and I was determined to see it through.

I flicked a hand through my curls, not wanting him to catch on to my sudden change in mood, not wanting him to guess I'd just sprung free of the spell. "Oh, well, I guess I must've missed him—what a shame!" I said, rearranging my expression to appear a tiny bit flustered. "Though I think I'll just make my way down real quick so I can have a look. Do you mind pointing me in the right direction?"

Dacian gaped, looked at me like I was stark-raving crazy. "The *ludus*?" He gasped. "Why, you can't go down there— it's dangerous!" He looked from me to the space just behind me, the space just to the right of me. Without even realizing it, he'd just answered my question, told me exactly which way to head.

"Oh, I suppose you're right." I giggled into my hand, and waved the thought away as though I'd already dismissed it. "Though I do need to find Messalina, so just give me a moment, and I'll find my way back—" I looked at him, looked right into his eyes, adding, "Promise you'll wait for me here?" Spinning on my heel before he had a chance to reply and heading in the direction he'd unknowingly sent me.

Aware of his voice calling out from behind me, letting me know he wasn't the least bit fooled by my story. "You really shouldn't go there, Aurelia," he said. "And believe me, you will *not* find Messalina there either. She is forbidden to go anywhere near the *ludus*—her uncle has made sure of that!"

A warning I was quick to ignore, already making my way down the stairs as I thought: *That's what you think, Dacian. That's what you think.*

9

I tore down the stairs, moving swiftly, quietly, hoping to gather as much information as I possibly could, knowing full well that Messalina couldn't be trusted—whatever she chose to reveal was carefully calculated and doled out in bits. She had an agenda—of that I was sure. And though I had no idea what that agenda might be, I did know that she didn't just control her world—she also controlled everyone in it—including, for a while anyway, me.

Pausing for a moment when my feet hit the landing, I stared down a long corridor crowded with big, hulking gladiator ghosts caught up in the same, lame routine as the last time I saw them. Their fists swinging wildly, their bodies slamming into each other—I swerved my way around them, clapped a hand over my nose to block out the stench, and kept going.

My eyes darting wildly, searching for signs of Messalina

or Theocoles—either would do—convinced that whichever one I found first, would lead me right to the other. I
moved among the row of cells, rising up on my toes in an
effort to peer into the small square openings marking the
top, though it wasn't until I reached the second to last one
that I saw them. Messalina looking so pristine, so perfectly
put together and groomed, she reminded me of a small,
delicate, porcelain doll that somehow wound up in a land-
fill—as a handsome, tunic-clad Theocoles stood just before
her—their bodies a mere razor's width apart as they gazed
longingly at each other.

I snapped my mouth shut before I could gasp, or squeal,
or do anything that might alert them to my presence, gaping
in wonder at the vision before me—the sight of it giving this
Soul Catch a whole new meaning.

Despite their vast and varied differences in stature and
class—despite their belonging to two different worlds—
Theocoles and Messalina had been in love. And from what I
could see, they still were.

But just when I thought I had it all figured out, Theocoles
shifted and revealed something new.

I leaned closer, my cheek pressed hard against the rough,
splintered wood, as I watched Theocoles shift to the side and
position himself, before springing into the air, his legs kicking,
sword slashing, piercing the air just beside where she stood.

And that's when I realized the rest of it—that's when I knew that while Messalina may have been gazing at him, Theocoles had not returned the look. He'd been staring right past her, still lost in his world.

But Messalina was not one to give up—she remained as stubborn as I knew her to be. And from the small square opening at the top of the door, I followed her progress as she eased her way around his thrusts and kicks, veering around him in a carefully choreographed dance.

Shouting as loud as she could, she fought to get the champion gladiator to take notice of her. Her voice fading, face growing increasingly frustrated, when he continued to ignore her in favor of his own tireless routine.

The scene so hopeless, dragging on for so long, I was just about to cut my losses and find my way back, when Messalina heaved a great sigh, found her way to the edge of his cot, where she sat, legs crossed daintily, hands folded primly, as she said, "Theocoles, I wish you would heed my words and please reconsider. You don't have to do this, you know. You don't have to go through with this. I will gladly give you the money, so that all of this madness can end."

Barely getting the words out before Theocoles stopped and turned, his gaze focused on hers, looking as though the light had come on, the fog had been cleared. He dropped his hands to his sides, leaned toward her, and said, "Your offer insults me—demeans me!" He shook his head, raked his fingers through his bangs, fixing his deep topaz eyes on hers. "Do you think me not worthy? Do you think I've come this far, slaughtered so many worthy opponents, only to make a spectacle of my own defeat?"

She looked at him, her face bearing so little expression, the words coming so quickly, so automatically I suddenly understood what was happening.

It was a performance.

They were both running lines from a scene they'd re-enacted countless times.

Theocoles so immersed in the role it was clear that for him, it was no different than the first time it happened. But for Messalina, the words were halfhearted, weary, spoken with no trace of emotion, like reading aloud from a textbook.

She'd tried to insert a new scene, tried to wake him up to a more modern day, but Theocoles remained stuck in a past he chose to live over and over again. Forcing Messalina to slip into the role she'd lived long ago in order to enjoy his attentions.

I pressed closer, strained to hear their words, knowing that if it was a scene he chose to relive then it was definitely a scene of great significance. It was not to be missed.

"You know I didn't mean it like that. I'm just anxious to begin our lives together," Messalina said, her voice soft and tired.

"As am I." He moved toward her, his gaze intense as he knelt down before her. "Everything I do is in anticipation of that day. Are you not aware of that?"

She cocked her head to the side and shot him a dubious look. "Everything you do is for me?" She pursed her lips, wrapped a loose curl around her index finger. "Are you quite sure of that? None of it is for Lucius?"

Theocoles paused, looked away, his face saddened, reflective, as he said, "There cannot be one without the other." He returned his gaze to hers. "I'm afraid our fates are all bound together." He reached toward her, brushed his finger across her brow, along the curve of her cheek, pressing the soft underside of her chin. He lifted her face until her gaze locked on his. "Now come, it is time we bid our goodbyes in favor of rest." He rose to his feet as she did the same. "My hope is that you will carry the sweet promise of our future straight into your dreams—and tomorrow, less than twenty-four hours from now, the world will be ours."

Messalina smiled bravely, swiped a quick hand across her cheek, halting the renegade tear that sped down her face before Theocoles could see it. Her expression stoic, resigned, she took a step toward him and grasped his hand in hers, as I pushed away from the door and raced back down the corridor as fast as I could.

10

Despite having retraced my same steps—the second I reached the landing I saw that my destination was not quite the one I expected.

Not even close.

Instead of the glamorous party I'd left, I found myself outside, squinting into a harsh, glaring sun, surrounded by hundreds—no scratch that—make that tens of thousands of toga-clad Romans, all of them pushing and shoving and fighting for someplace to sit.

"Aurelia!" A familiar voice rang out from behind me, as I gazed all around in confusion. "Aurelia, what on earth are you doing out here among the common masses?"

I felt a tug on the back of my dress, and turned to find Messalina smiling before me, her face radiant, her cheeks flushed the same light pink as the gorgeous new gown that she wore.

"If you're done acquainting yourself with the lower classes, perhaps we can move on to my uncle's box where it's far less crowded, and far more welcoming with its abundance of food and drink and more importantly in this heat—shade!" She rolled her eyes and laughed, retrieving a gold-and-pink fan from the folds of her dress. She waved it under my chin in an effort to cool me. "Oh, and you might also like to know that Dacian has been making himself quite crazy, wondering if you'll make an appearance—worried he might never get to see you again. I hear you've been quite naughty, playing hard to get." She shot me a sly look, before she went on. "Truly, the boy is in a very sorry state. He just won't let up! Keeps insisting I tell him whether or not he can expect you. Though I must say it's been such great fun watching the poor boy suffer, I refuse to divulge much of anything." She lifted her fan to her face, hiding all but her eyes. "It seems he's quite smitten with you, now, isn't he? The question is, what are you going to do about it? Are you smitten as well? C'mon, you can tell me, Aurelia—do you feel the same way as he?"

She looked at me, eyes shining, face beaming, waiting for an answer that never really came. I was too busy trying to figure out what had just happened—how the night had turned so swiftly to day—how I'd found my way to the Colosseum without even realizing it.

Though Messalina didn't seem the slightest bit bothered by my silence, she just smiled brightly, crooked her arm in offering, and beckoned for me to follow alongside her.

Her smile plastered to her face, refusing to fade even after I said, "No." I crossed my arms before me and shook my head for emphasis, causing my thick blond curls to brush against my cheeks. "I need to find Theocoles—as you well know." I stared at her in challenge, noting the way her brow shot halfway up her forehead as her lips quirked to the side.

"Well, of course you'll see Theocoles," she said, her voice light but forced, her eyes moving over me slowly, conducting a very thorough inventory. "Don't be silly, Aurelia—he's the main attraction, is he not?" She shook her head and *tsked*, her tongue tapping the roof of her mouth. "Everyone will see him today, to be sure. After all, he is the reason we're all here. Though I'm afraid you may have a bit of a wait; he's not scheduled to fight until later in the day. So come now, enough of this nonsense." She tilted her head to the side and offered her hand, fingers beckoning as she said, "Why don't you join me?" But when I didn't, when I didn't make a move either way, she leaned closer, her voice lowered to a whisper. "Oh, you're right. Before we get to all that we really must attend to your dress. Perhaps you need a little freshening up, no? After all, Dacian is in quite a stir, and we don't want to disappoint him, now, do we?"

I gazed down the front of my dress, noting that, yeah, it was a little wrinkled, a bit dust covered from my time spent in the *ludus*, a little bit the worse for wear, but still nowhere near as tragic as she seemed to think. But just as I started to protest that I was just fine, that I wasn't about to follow her anywhere until she explained a few things, she looked at me with those warm brown eyes, lifted a cool hand to my brow and brushed a finger lightly against it, and the next thing I knew I was agreeing to it all. The dress, the hair, the jewels, the luxurious box that her uncle owned, which also, according to Messalina, was the best, most important, most comfortable, most sought-after spot for viewing the games.

"You should consider yourself quite lucky to sit there," she said.

And the thing is, I did feel lucky. I felt really, really incredibly lucky, in more ways than one. Every single thing that had once been missing from my afterlife was now in my grasp.

I'd been longing for a good friend, a friend so close we were like sisters—and I'd found one in Messalina.

I'd been longing for a chance at a bit of fun and romance, and because of Messalina, I'd found it in Dacian.

I was one of the privileged few. I was lucky, lucky, lucky. My life was wonderfully good. And it was all because of *her*.

The moment we entered the box, Messalina let go of

my arm and hung back. Watching with an amused smile as Dacian rushed toward me, went about the whole bowing/ hand-kissing ritual, before leading me to the seat beside his, where I pretended to listen as he chatted on and on about the day's program.

There were wild-game hunts in the works, a group of prisoners to be executed, and bippidy blah blah, on and on he went. Having no idea that I was well beyond caring—immersed in a land where the only things that interested me were how amazing I looked in my new lavender dress—and how amazing I felt whenever Dacian's eyes flitted toward mine.

"And then of course once that's all said and done then it's time for the great Theocoles, who's set to defend his title as the Pillar of Doom. As I mentioned last night, this may well turn out to be his very last fight. I suspect that's why the Colosseum is filled to capacity—he's a very big draw. Many of the spectators have already placed their bets on his fate, and I must admit, you can count me among them. In fact . . ."

His words faded, edged out by the one that continued to play in my head: *Theocoles.*

Why did the name hold such importance?

Why should I even care about the fate of some gladiator slave who could very well be facing his final day?

I leaned back in my seat, confused by the way the name made me feel.

"Did you say it was his . . . last fight?" I turned toward Dacian, aware of a vague yet insistent nudge coming from someplace deep within me, egging me on.

Dacian nodded. "Theocoles has more than just his life riding on this fight—and no matter the outcome, it promises to be quite a spectacle, indeed." He lowered his voice conspiratorially, caught up in the excitement of being the first to inform me. "He's garnered himself quite the fan club, as you will soon see. And it's not just because the stakes are so high, but because he knows how to put on a show. In just a short amount of time he's learned how to win over the crowd. Theocoles discovered early on that an important part of a gladiator's survival is not just skill with a sword and a drive to conquer and win—but also to ensure that the crowd stays entertained. It's not enough just to slay your opponent—the crowd will tire of that rather quickly. Blood and gore—blood and gore . . ." He made a bored face. "As you will see, by the time all the ravaged carcasses are dragged from the arena, the crowd will have already witnessed several hours of slaughter, and after a while, one grisly battle can begin to fade into the next. A real gladiator, a champion gladiator such as Theocoles, remains well aware of this fact, and therefore they take it among themselves to choreograph their battles to provide maximum entertainment, to ensure the crowd's attention stays riveted on them."

I hung on his every word, committing it to memory as I struggled to take it all in. The intense look in my eye causing Dacian to say, "Oh no." He shook his head in mock horror. "I can see I've said too much. I can see it in the gleam in your eyes, your heart is already captured, and now it's just a matter of time before I'll be forced to throw myself into the arena in order to win your affections!"

He laughed when he said it, but somehow the joke washed right over me. For some strange reason I chose to take his words seriously. "What? No!" I shook my head, caught off guard by—well, by just about everything. "Please, you must not do so on my account," I added, the words awkward, stumbling right out of my mouth.

"Don't do what on your account?" Messalina crept up from behind me, her movement fluid, catlike, grinning in a way that left me wondering just how long she might've been listening as she draped herself over the back of my chair.

"It seems I've made the mistake of getting Aurelia a little too well-versed in the games. She's obsessed, I can tell. He has yet to appear in the arena, and already I have lost her to the legend that is Theocoles."

"Aw, the Pillar of Doom." Messalina laughed, though the sound was not light, and her eyes failed to shine.

"You said he was set to go free?" I leaned toward Dacian. "Does this have something to do with Lucius?"

Dacian looked confused, though he was nowhere near as confused as I felt. *Where had the name come from? What was I even talking about?*

Just as the memory began to resurface, a fleeting glimpse of the conversation I witnessed between Messalina and Theocoles in his cell when I'd first heard the name— Messalina tapped me lightly on the shoulder and said, "If Theocoles shall be crowned today's victor, his winnings will be enough to cover the gambling debts Lucius owes, which in turn will secure Lucius' freedom, as he currently works in the quarries, a horrible fate to be sure." She rubbed her arms, gave a little shiver, though her eyes never left mine. "It will also conclude the contract Theocoles holds with my uncle, which in turn will free him as well. It is a very important day for both of them, indeed."

"So that means Theocoles *volunteered*?" My eyes met Messalina's as a new understanding began to take shape. "And that's why you . . ."

"That's why I *what*?" she said, and the moment her eyes met mine, I was no longer sure. What was crystal clear a moment before had vanished just as quickly.

Dacian's voice cutting into my cloudy, vague thoughts when he said, "His brother got in a bit over his head." He scoffed, made a face, leaving no doubt as to how he felt about that.

His actions causing Messalina to stiffen beside me, as I remained parked between them, aware of something stirring inside me, poking, prodding, fighting to get my attention, and yet my head felt so foggy, all I could do was run my hands over the deep lavender folds of my dress and lose myself in admiring it.

"Theocoles has shown nothing but the greatest honor and bravery," Messalina said, her voice laced with an edge that was impossible to miss. "His brother Lucius means everything to him, and what Theocoles has been able to accomplish on his brother's behalf is nothing short of greatness. And I, for one, believe he should be commended for that. No matter how this day ends, he shall not be forgotten, for surely that would be considered no less than a crime."

"Tell you what—if he *lives*, I'll be the first to commend him," Dacian said, paying no mind to Messalina's tone, much less the stricken expression his words left on her face. "And if not . . ." He grinned, glancing between the two of us as he slid a finger clean across the width of his neck.

"Well, we'll just have to wait and see then, won't we?" Messalina's eyes darted between us, her response eliciting a sarcastic chuckle from Dacian, and silence from me.

I was gone.

Lost in a fog I couldn't even begin to work my way through.

Feeling torn, pulled in two different directions, as though caught in the middle of some crazy, invisible tug-of-war, with no way of knowing who pulled at my strings, much less which side I should favor.

"Aurelia? Are you okay?" Messalina leaned toward me, her face a mask of concern.

Aurelia. That was me. That's what everyone called me.

Or was it? I was no longer sure.

Messalina placed a finger under my chin and lifted it toward hers as she gazed directly into my eyes. Fussing at my hair, pretending to rearrange a stray curl, she brushed a cool finger across the width of my brow—the feel of her touch instantly lifting the fog, allowing the sun to break through, as everything sprang back into view.

"Are you okay?" she repeated, her gaze fixed on mine.

I gazed all around, taking in the enormity of the arena, the tens of thousands of cheering spectators—sure that each and every one of them would do anything to trade places with me. Sure that each and every one of them longed to claim a place among such luxury and comfort—surrounded by mountains of food, an endless supply of drink, keeping company with rich and entitled Roman nobility—not to mention the insanely cute boy who sat right beside me.

I returned my gaze to hers, my voice filled with the extent of my gratitude when I said, "Everything's great. Everything's just absolutely perfect. And I have you to thank."

I I

I watched the procession that marked the start of the games in confusion. Surprised by the way the crowd remained strangely quiet, almost solemn, until Dacian explained how that would soon change. It was merely the official portion of the day, he told me. The time when weapons were inspected, a dead emperor was remembered, and the gladiators were all introduced—allowing the crowd a chance to take them all in, knowing full well that by the day's end more than half of them would never stand again.

When it was over, the gates dragged open once more, setting a pack of ferocious jungle cats loose in the arena. At first roaring in fear, unsure what to make of their new surroundings, it wasn't long before they adapted, their instincts kicked in, and they busied themselves with stalking their prey—devouring one poor, unfortunate prisoner after another.

The crowd cheered in response, stomping and clapping in glee as they watched a succession of people get shredded and gutted and ripped into small, bloodied bits—pitted in a fight they could never, ever win.

That same cheering failing to cease when those very same cats were later hunted and killed by gladiators who specialized in such skills.

Until finally—after hours of unrelenting blood and gore—after hours of watching unfathomable death and violence—it was time for the gladiators to take center stage. And I found myself so desensitized by that point, so completely unshakable, it wasn't long before I became as entranced as any other spectator—cheering and jeering right along with them.

Giving thumbs up whenever a battle was tied, and I found both parties worthy of living—giving thumbs down when I wasn't entertained quite enough, when I demanded someone be held accountable for the lack—to die a grisly death to atone for my boredom.

Sometimes shouting, "Live!" other times shouting, "Kill!" depending on my mood. I was consumed with the power I held. Aware that I was only one among many, that in the end, it was the emperor's decision to grant life or death, and yet, was he not bound to the whims of his subjects? Was he not swayed by their need to be appeased from the drudgery of their lives with a show of *bread and circus*?

I reveled in being part of that decision, in knowing my vote helped to decide just who was allowed to live another day—and just who was sentenced to die.

And when the heavy iron gates swung wide once again, and Theocoles thundered into the arena, it quickly became clear why he was so favored.

Theocoles didn't walk, neither did he run, but rather he strutted, sauntered—arms raised high above his head, his sword and shield waving in acknowledgment of his fifty thousand most admiring fans, leaving no doubt that he loved them, just as much as they loved him.

The stadium practically shaking with the rumble of stomping feet and clapping hands, I watched as Theocoles turned, acknowledging every section of the stadium, circling the wave of praise much as the earth circles the warmth of the sun.

The applause significantly dimming when his opponent, Urbicus, entered to a chorus of hisses and boos—and though he appeared equally strong, equally fierce, equally determined to hold up his end—it was clear from the start that he lacked the innate fire and charisma of the champion gladiator, and because of it, the crowd would never be swayed to his side. He just couldn't compete with Theocoles' unique brand of magnetism—his deadly combination of bravery, skill, showmanship, and undeniable movie star appeal.

Much like everyone around me, I slid to the edge of my seat, watching in fascination, captivated as the battle began. Urbicus putting up a very good fight, though not good enough—he spent most of his energy deflecting Theocoles' well-aimed blows that left him so bloodied and battered, his strength quickly seeped out of him, while Theocoles raged on, his own wounds appearing shallow and superficial at most.

Despite his rival's weakening state—despite Theocoles' numerous chances to lead Urbicus to his final rest—the battle waged on, and on, and on—with Theocoles refusing to end it, determined to give the crowd what they came for, and more. He continued to pounce, and leap, and inflict wound after gaping wound upon his victim until Urbicus' skin resembled a fringe of blood-soaked ribbons.

I watched in a combination of amazement and revulsion, wondering at which point Theocoles would decide to end it so he could collect his winnings, thereby freeing his brother, and himself. Yet I was so caught up in the spectacle, I dreaded the moment it would end.

I leaned into Dacian, so overcome with excitement and nerves, too busy watching Theocoles slice his opponent to shreds, it was a moment before I noticed our shoulders were pressed snugly together.

"Why doesn't he just kill him already and get it over with, so he can claim his victory?" I asked.

My gaze darting between Dacian and the arena, suddenly aware that he'd taken my hand, laced his fingers with mine as he said, "Worried about Theocoles, are you?" His voice teased at my ear as he leaned even closer. "Not to worry—he's just doing what he does best. He's playing the crowd. He's giving us the show that he's known for, and it hasn't failed him yet." He motioned toward the arena, where Theocoles, having removed his studded steel helmet and tossed it aside, shook his long, shaggy hair in acknowledgment of his tens of thousands of roaring fans. "He's addicted to the applause. Needs it as much as a flower needs rain. He knows this is it. He's all too aware that after today he'll never again claim center stage. They'll talk about him for a while, recount each move of his victory, but soon enough their attentions will begin to wane, just like they always do. And, once that happens, it won't be long until the memory of Theocoles fades into oblivion, as another champion rises up in his place. And, despite what Messalina prefers to think, one day the great champion, the Pillar of Doom, will be reduced to nothing more than a ghost of a memory, with no lasting proof that he ever existed. I'm sure on some level, Theocoles is all too aware of that, and so, it's for that very reason that he's determined to milk it—to glean all from this moment that he possibly can."

"*Milk it?*" I peered at Dacian, struggling to decide why I was so struck by the phrase, especially with all the other things that were happening. A boy was holding my hand! There was major bloodshed in the arena! Still, his words nudged at me, they just didn't blend, didn't quite mesh with the kinds of words he usually used.

Dacian looked at me. Assuming I didn't understand its meaning, he said, "I mean he wants to seize the moment— he wants to squeeze it for all that it's worth. Much as one might squeeze a goat's udder for its milk—"

"Got it," I said, stealing a chance to remove my hand from his. I was suddenly jumpy, testy, something nudging at the edge of my memory, though I had no idea what it could be, no idea why I was feeling that way.

The crowd roared, dragging my attention back to the arena, eager to catch up on all that I'd missed. Watching as Theocoles loped around its perimeter, sword and shield out-stretched to either side—proving that, once again, Dacian was right. Theocoles loved the adulation. Thrived on it from what I could see. He was definitely *milking it*, to be sure. He wouldn't go easily.

I glanced around the box, noting how, just like me, everyone else was on the edge of their seats, including the emperor, who'd pushed aside his heaping platter of wine and grapes in order to direct his full attention to the games, while Messalina's uncle, the owner of the *ludus*, the owner of Theocoles, stood off to his side, mumbling a long stream of words under his breath that I couldn't quite hear.

Though when I looked at Messalina, I couldn't help but notice how her reaction differed from the rest. While everyone else was in full-on nail-biting mode, she'd already turned away, refusing to look. Despite the fact that aside from Lucius and Theocoles, she had the most riding on the outcome.

Though a moment later when Dacian reached for my hand, the thought slipped away. The only thing I was conscious of was the tentative way his fingers laced with mine as his face veered close, then closer still as he said, "He's getting ready. It's almost over. And trust me, you will not want to miss this."

We rose to our feet, everyone did. A crowd of people all pushing forward, straining to get a better look as Theocoles finally turned his back on the crowd and approached his severely wounded opponent, who, despite the grave condition he was in, despite the fact that he could barely gather enough strength to stand, refused to fall. All too aware that imminent death was well on its way, he was determined to die nobly, bravely, a death worthy of a gladiator. He would not give in without one final fight.

"Kill!" I yelled, following the lead of the crowd, my

thumb pointing down as did Dacian's beside me. The word shouted over and over again in one long, rhythmic chant—the soundtrack of a bloodthirsty crowd.

Theocoles turned, letting us know he'd acknowledged the word, and that he planned to oblige us at the first sign of the emperor's bidding.

But while Theocoles was facing us, his opponent had taken the opportunity to regroup, to make one last stab at victory, or at least die trying.

Stumbling forward, he used whatever remaining strength he had to take one last, wild swing with his blade. Its sharp, pointed edge clipping Theocoles at the back of his knees where it sliced wide and deep. Causing him to stagger, to sag toward the sand, his sword and shield having slipped from his fingers, abandoned at his side.

His hands grasped at the air as he tilted erratically, body swaying, face bearing an expression of unmistakable shock when he found himself falling, collapsing, his once cele-brated form no more than a bloody, lame heap.

The crowd hushed into a strange, eerie silence, needing a moment to adapt to such an unexpected turn of events, as I did the same. My hand clamped over my mouth, unable to believe what I saw unfolding before me, vaguely aware of Dacian sliding a comforting arm around my waist.

We moved forward, rushed to the edge of the box, as

did everyone around us—Rome's finest all bunched up together, eyes bulging, necks craning, eager to see what terrible, unexpected thing might happen next.

Theocoles struggled to rise, but his wounds were too deep, his muscles now sliced in half were no longer working. He fell onto his back, staring in complete disbelief as his battered and bloodied opponent towered over him with his sword raised high, ready, willing, waiting for that one simple word that would allow him to claim certain victory by plunging it deep into Theocoles' throat.

Not expecting Theocoles to turn, to use whatever strength he had left to roll onto his side—his eyes frantically searching for Messalina's—longing to apologize, to say a final goodbye.

That one single look containing so much longing, so much meaning, so much regret, I couldn't stop the crystalline tears that rolled down my cheeks.

But the crowd failed to see what I saw.

They misread the whole thing.

Knowing only that Theocoles had turned his back on his opponent, they mistook his final goodbye for an act of cowardice.

Furious to learn that the man they once held as their hero was neither noble enough, nor brave enough, to face his own death (an act that could not, would not be tolerated—

an act that went against everything a gladiator stood for), they were quick to turn against him.

Tens of thousands of mouths that just a moment ago had hung silent in shock, were now fueled with revenge, shouting the verdict of: "*Kill!*" over and over again.

The demand so overwhelming, so all consuming, the emperor was quick to nod his consent.

The crowd pressed tighter, causing my head to grow foggy as I gasped for each breath. Swallowing mouthfuls of air only to realize I didn't exhale.

I had no need of it—no need to breathe.

A vague awareness of something tugging at the edge of my memory—something about me—about Theocoles— though I had no idea what it could be.

While my fellow Romans were absorbed with the arena, eager to see the mighty Theocoles, the Pillar of Doom, meet his end, I turned toward Messalina, looking for guidance, hoping she might be able to tell me why I was no longer dependent on air.

But Messalina was gone. And as I stared hard at the space where she stood, the fog cleared, and I was sprung from my trance.

12

I slipped away from Dacian, pushed past the Roman nobles standing before me, and leaped as high as I could. Immune to the sound of Dacian's frantic voice calling out from behind me, I gripped the sides of my gown, bunched it up in my hands, and hurtled right over the edge of the box. Landing on the shoulders of a startled, and not so happy toga-clad man, I evaded his angry, outstretched hands, and found my way to the ground. Winding my way to the center of the arena where I glanced between a headless Theocoles lying prone on the sand, and the completely intact, somewhat filmier version that stood alongside him, staring down at his former body in a mixture of loss and confusion.

"Theocoles." I tugged hard on his hand, knowing I had to move fast. I had no idea where Messalina might've gone, but I could only assume she wouldn't stay gone for too long. "Theocoles, please, you've got to listen to me. You've got to realize that you're dead. It's over. The battle was lost and there is no going back. And while I'm truly sorry for what happened to you, that you had to die in such a totally gruesome, violent way, it's time for you to put all of that behind you and move on. There's a better place for you—a much better place, where you belong. And if you'll just allow me to—"

He turned toward me, his deep topaz eyes staring hard into mine, as though he really did see me, as though he really did hear me—and while my face beamed with victory, I decided to save the celebration for later. First, I had to see this thing through.

"Who is that?" he asked, his voice like a whisper as he gazed down at his poor mangled body.

"It's you," I told him, my voice equally soft, sympathetic, knowing firsthand just how shocking it can be to see such a thing, to make the transition between life and death. "That's what happened to your body. And while I'm truly sorry for that, as you can see, the most essential part of you continues to exist. It's not over for you, Theocoles, not even close."

He moved toward his corpse, kneeling beside it as I did the same. Though unlike him, I did my best not to look at it, and I definitely didn't touch it like he did—it was way too gruesome to even consider. I may have been enthralled with all the blood and gore when I was Aurelia, but returned to myself, I was not only grossed out, but deeply ashamed by the way I'd gotten so easily sucked in—they way I'd so eagerly shouted "Live!" and "Kill!" along with the rest of them. I promised myself I wouldn't let that happen again.

I mean, seriously, it was pretty much the kind of thing you see in horror movies—the kind of movies that, when I was alive anyway, I was forbidden to watch. My parents assuring me that I was too young, that I'd be haunted by nightmares, and yet, since the moment I became a Soul Catcher I'd been forced to witness all manner of grisly, gory gruesomeness—the kind of stuff that pushed my gag reflex beyond all reasonable limits.

That's it, I thought. *As soon as this business with Theocoles is over, I'm scheduling a nice, long talk with the Council about more age-appropriate assignments!*

Though it was only a second later when I remembered how I found myself there—I was the one who practically begged for more difficult Soul Catches.

"Be careful what you wish for," my mom used to say. And when I gazed down at the disgusting, headless body before me I knew it was true.

Theocoles turned away from his corpse and gazed after his opponent. Watching as Urbicus was practically dragged from the arena, left in such a sorry state I couldn't help but think he was moments away from meeting his own afterlife.

"And what becomes of him?" Theocoles mumbled, almost as though speaking to himself.

I glanced between the two of them, shrugging as I said, "He'll succumb to his own death eventually. And from the looks of it, I'd guess sooner rather than later. In the end, no matter how hard we may try to avoid it, all of us go. The body is temporary, but the soul never dies."

I sat back in surprise, realizing that for probably the first time ever, my words didn't contain even a trace of the grudge I once used to hold over my own early demise. I was just stating the facts as I knew them, without any of my usual animosity. I'd finally reached the point where I no longer took my death personally.

"Where are the roses?" he asked, brows merging in confusion as he glanced from the crowd to the sand that, instead of the flowers he was used to, was scattered with chunks of skin and blood, and gawd knows what else. "They always throw roses. The crowd loves me and that's how they show their love for me. They shower me with rose petals, thousands and thousands of red rose petals that I collect in my hands and crush into my palms, so that I can carry the scent back into the barracks with me and relive the memory."

"Sorry," I said. "I guess they forgot." Wondering if I should try to manifest some rose petals real quick so I could spread them about and make him feel better, then quickly decided against it.

It was better not to coddle him. Better for him to face the facts, no matter how brutal. Facing the truth was an important part of the process. It would help him move on, something he desperately needed to do—sooner rather than later if I had any say in it.

"They have turned against me." His eyes grew wide, frantic, as the reality of his situation sank in. "I have lost their adoration—their favor!" He gazed around wildly as though searching for a way to remedy it. "I am their champion—their Pillar of Doom—how dare they forget that?"

His voice cracked as he jumped to his feet. Retrieving his helmet, he waved it at the crowd in an effort to get their attention, before he jammed it back onto his head.

"I will win them back! I will regain their favor! If it is the last thing I do, I will hear the roar of their approval—I will bask in the thunder of their applause once again!"

Oh boy.

I got to my feet and stood alongside him, saying, "Uh, Theocoles, seriously, you really need to rethink this." I reached toward him, my hand grasping, reaching, only to watch in astonishment as he moved right past me, kicked a cloud of sand right into my face as he reached for his sword, and slumped into a crouching position.

"Okay, you know what?" I scowled, clearing my face and

dress of disgusting, bloody, squishy chunks of I-don't-want-to-know-what. "That's *enough*! I mean it. I don't care who you think you are—I don't care if you're the champion of this arena—I don't care if you're the champion of the whole entire world—you *cannot* kick sand in my face! Really, I am so not joking. I don't care what time you come from, I don't care that you're used to living like a barbarian, it is absolutely, positively, not okay to disregard me like that! Do you hear me?" I placed my hands on my hips, and waited for a reply. Directing the question at him once again when I shouted, "I said: *Do. You. Hear. Me*?"

His eyes met mine, and in that moment I knew I'd connected. I knew I'd finally broken through to him.

Theocoles had heard me.

He'd seen me.

I'd just accomplished what no other Soul Catcher before me was able to do.

I'd broken him free of his trance.

I moved toward him, my palm open in offering, reaching for his. Knowing it was just a matter of time before I made that glistening golden veil that would lead him to the bridge, to where he belonged.

My voice choked with the thrill of victory, I gazed into his eyes and said, "Theocoles, come. It is time for you to move on."

13

Theocoles leaned forward, his fingers flexing, straining, moving toward . . . his sword.

First he grabbed his sword.

Then he reached for his shield.

I stood there, gaping in a mixture of confused outraged indignation when Messalina appeared.

"We've been over this, Riley. Theocoles hears only what he chooses to hear. And, just so you know, when he finally does break out of his spell, it won't be because of *you*. It will be because of *me*."

She moved toward me, a vision in pink with a feral smile that widened her cheeks, as a savage gleam shone in her eye.

And all I could think was: *Run! Resist! Do not let her touch you! Do not let her enchant you again!*

But it was no use.

Well before I could move, well before I could get my

body in cahoots with my head, she leaned toward me, her long, cool fingers sweeping the space just north of my brow, once again pretending to tame a stray curl that had fallen out of place.

And the next thing I knew I was standing in the middle of a loud and crowded room. My cheeks flushed, my gaze shyly avoiding that of a very cute boy who grasped hold of my hand.

A boy who introduced himself as Dacian.

A boy who seemed to think my name was Aurelia.

And maybe it was. I couldn't be sure, when there was no one around to dispute it.

"Why have I not seen you before?" he asked, his eyes shining with unrestrained interest.

I ducked my head, gazed up at him through my tangle of lashes, my voice bearing the full extent of my confusion when I said, "But you have." Only to watch him shake his head and immediately discard what I said.

"Trust me, I would not have forgotten such a thing. There is no way such a beauty as yours would ever escape me."

Me? A beauty?

I gazed down at myself, smoothed my palms down the front of my gown, shocked to see I possessed the kind of body that I once only dreamed of. And if the heft and weight of the blond curls that bounced on my shoulders was anything to go by, then chances were I just might be as beautiful and radiant as the lavender dress that I wore.

I leaned over, peering into the elaborate, tiered fountain beside me, greedily searching for a trace of my own reflection, and relaxing when I found my face beaming back in a series of ripples. The image unsteady, wavering, but still confirming Dacian's words to be true.

And yet, if what Dacian said was true—if my name really was Aurelia—if I really was a beautiful, teenaged girl—then why did it all feel so strange?

Why did it all seem so unreal, like some kind of dream?

The boy—the body—the face—the dress—the strange-sounding name which he called me—it all seemed as unstable as the image I'd seen in the fountain.

It must be the party. It must be the large crowd of people and all of the noise that went with it. I wasn't used to such things. I wasn't used to feeling so cramped, and hemmed in. I needed air, needed the night sky, along with the stars, and the moon, and all that went with it.

"I trust I can leave you in Dacian's care?" Messalina smiled, her gaze dancing between us.

I blinked. Wondering where she had come from. I didn't remember seeing her arrive. It was as though she'd appeared out of nowhere.

"I trust that I can count on Dacian to be on his very best

behavior when I leave my dearest friend in his care?"

Messalina and I were friends. Right. It was all becoming clear. We were good friends. Best friends. She lent me the dress, along with the jewelry I wore. She even fixed my hair, pinned it with jewels—the two of us such close friends we were almost like sisters.

"*Don't go!*" I said. Or at least I tried to say it, but the words refused to cooperate, and were instantly replaced with, "I assure you I will be fine. If Dacian dares to get the slightest bit out of hand, I will summon one of the gladiators to take care of him." I smiled flirtatiously, my eyes shining with laughter as I glanced between them. "In fact,"—I made a point of pouting prettily— "I will do one better than that. I will choose that giant, hulking gladiator right over there." I pointed toward the opposite side of the room, where the tallest, most fierce, most handsome gladiator stood with his hands and legs shackled to those who stood alongside him, ensuring they wouldn't do anything reckless, ensuring the partygoers, the finest of Roman nobility, did not experience a repeat of the legendary revolt that was once led by Spartacus. "I will elicit the help of the one they call the Pillar of Doom. I think the threat alone is likely to keep Dacian subdued, no?" I shot him an inviting smile, eager to hear his reply.

"You would sic Theocoles on me?" Dacian said, his face a

mask of mock horror as Messalina giggled beside him.

Theocoles.

What was it about that name that made me feel so odd inside?

I glanced at Messalina, my friend, my dearest friend, then shaking my head, I rid myself of any lingering doubts as I grasped her hand in mine and said, "Go! Go check in with your aunt, please. I am sure that with the threat of Theocoles hanging over him—" I paused on the name, had to force myself to move on. "Well, I'm sure Dacian can be counted on to behave now, can't he?"

Dacian laughed in a way that made his eyes shine, as Messalina leaned between us, trailing a finger first along Dacian's brow and then mine. "Actually," she said, her face gone suddenly serious. "I'm counting on both of you to be on your best behavior, and I'm sure you will not disappoint me." Then she turned on her heel, and left us alone.

14

"Shall we?" Dacian gestured toward a large platter of sweets a servant was offering.

But I just shook my head. I was in no mood for sweets. Not when I longed for fresh air, night sky, and escape.

"I think I'd rather go outside for a bit," I said, my voice light and girlish but serious all the same. "I think I'd like some fresh air."

Dacian nodded, offered his arm, and when I crooked my own around it, he led me through a series of crowded rooms until we found ourselves standing on a balcony that overlooked the arena where the gladiators trained during the day.

"Look at all the stars!" I leaned my head back, my complicated arrangement of curls and twists cascading to my waist as I took in the magnificent expanse of black sky.

"Do you know the constellations?" Dacian asked.

I smiled, admitting that while I did indeed know most of them, I still wanted him to show me.

"Well, let's see then . . ." He squinted into the dark. "Right there is Cassiopeia." He pointed, then moving his finger he said, "And that over there is Draco, of course. And, if I'm not mistaken, that one right there would be Aurelia Major." He turned to me, his hair falling over one eye.

"Aurelia Major?" I shook my head and laughed. "And just when exactly was that one discovered? It's the first I've heard of it."

"Oh, it's quite real, I assure you." He smiled, exposing teeth so white, dimples so deep, and a face so cute, I felt as though a bubble of butterflies had just burst in my chest. "How shall I prove it?"

The question hung between us, a flirtatious challenge that I had no idea how to respond to. All I knew is that if I didn't do something, if I didn't speak up, if I didn't look away, perhaps even move away, then Dacian would soon kiss me.

And while I wasn't entirely sure that I wanted him to kiss me—I also wasn't entirely sure that I was willing to miss out on what might be my one and only chance at him kissing me.

He rubbed his lips together, steadied his shaky fingers on my arm, then closed his eyes and leaned toward me, as I stood there before him, body rigid, mind busily taking note of every tiny detail, knowing that later, I'd want to review them.

Noting the distant sounds of laughter drifting behind us—the swishy sound of my dress when Dacian moved his hand from my arm to my waist and pulled me closer to him. And then, before I could note anything further, his lips had found mine—pressing briefly—once—twice—and then he pulled away again.

Dacian grinned, slid his arm around me, and returned to stargazing—the silence unfolding between us until it felt as wide as the sky. But instead of rushing to fill it, I let it unfurl. Words would be said eventually, but for the moment, I was determined to savor the quiet for as long as it stood.

"Look!" Dacian's voice was edged with excitement as his finger pointed toward the sky. "There's Aurelia Minor! Right there—right next to Aurelia Major! Now do you believe me?" His gaze met mine, and I saw in his eyes the same thing that I felt deep inside.

We liked each other. There was no way to hide it.

I averted my gaze, suddenly overcome by shyness, having no clue what to say. Wondering if I should maybe tease him about failing to act on his best behavior—that the brief kiss we shared was more than enough to make good on my threat to summon a gladiator. Though I quickly decided against it, worried that he might take me seriously—that it might give him reason not to kiss me again—something I was not willing to risk.

"Are you cold?" He smoothed a hand over my bare arm in an effort to warm me.

"A little." I shrugged, unaware that I'd shivered until he'd just mentioned it.

He looked at me, his gaze gone all fuzzy like he might try to kiss me again. But just as he started, I glimpsed something shiny, something dazzling, something spectacular and fleeting, shooting clear across the sky.

And as I turned my head to get a better look, Dacian moved in for the kiss, resulting in two noses that smacked hard together as I said, "Look, a shooting . . . *star* . . ."

We stepped away from each other, gasping in shock and embarrassment that soon gave way to an uncontrollable fit of giggles. The two of us falling all over each other, falling all over ourselves, hands carefully cupped to our faces, checking for damage, the sight of which only fueled a whole new set of giggles that completely consumed us.

Our laughter halted by the sound of someone saying, "Hi. Uh, sorry to bother you, but I was wondering if you might be able to help me?"

I turned, my hand instantly dropping from my nose to my side as I took in the stranger before me. My eyes grazing over his longish flop of brown hair that swooped over his brow before falling into a remarkable pair of green eyes framed by a thick set of lashes. Working my way all the way down a set of very strange, entirely unfamiliar clothes that clearly marked him as a foreigner—including a pair of shoes that were big and clumsy and miles away from the strappy leather sandals all the other males wore. And when I worked my way back up, I saw that he chewed some sort of odd green object lodged in the side of his mouth, which just made him look even more odd than he already did. Everything about him was weird—and yet, somehow I found that I couldn't turn away no matter how hard I tried.

Dacian moved before me, as though to protect me—a move I found rather sweet, if not also a tad bit unnecessary. "And just what is it you need help with?" He gave the stranger a once-over almost as thorough as mine.

"I'm trying to locate a . . . friend." The stranger's voice was cautious, careful. "I'm afraid I'm responsible for her, and I'm wondering if either of you might've seen her. She's blond, blue-eyed, and at twelve years old she's a bit on the small side. Goes by the name of—"

I slipped back to Dacian's side, my eyes meeting the stranger's, unsure what to make of the unmistakable way he was looking at me.

With shock.

And disbelief.

As though he wasn't just looking *at* me, but also *through* me, *beyond* me—and while I had no idea what he saw, there was no denying his interest was piqued.

"*Riley?*" His voice croaked as the straw fell from his mouth and landed at his feet. He stepped forward, his gait tentative, a bit shaky, stopping when Dacian raised a hand between them, flashing his palm in warning.

"I'm going to have to stop you right there," Dacian said, the threat implied in his tone. "Clearly you have the wrong party, so it's best you move on."

If the stranger heard, he chose to ignore it. And though he made no further move in my direction, that didn't stop him from staring in complete and utter fascination when he said, "Riley? Riley Bloom? Tell me, does that name mean anything to you?"

Heat rose to my cheeks, as a familiar feeling blossomed inside me—and though I knew I should look away, I just couldn't, I was frozen in place

"It's like I said." Dacian took another step toward him. "You have the wrong party. There is no . . . *Riley Bloom* here." He stumbled over the name. "It's time for you to move on."

The stranger glanced between us, his gaze landing on mine, holding the look for so long I couldn't help but squirm under the weight of it.

Aware of Dacian's body tensing, his fingers curling into fists, refusing to relax even after the stranger said, "No worries, I'm leaving." He turned, stepped away, glancing over his shoulder to add, "At least for now anyway."

15

Messalina and I stayed up late into the night, picking at a tray of leftover sweets, braiding each other's hair, and swapping tales that we swore into the strictest confidence, requiring a solemn vow of secrecy before they were told. And after I'd listened to her gush on and on about her top-secret romance with Theocoles, it was my turn to relate every last detail of the moment Dacian kissed me.

"He did *not!*" Messalina plopped a sweet into her mouth and leaned toward me as her eyes grew wide with surprise.

"He did, indeed." I smiled at the memory. "Not much of a gentleman to be sure, but still, I decided not to call him on it. In fact, I even let him do it again!"

"No!" Messalina laughed and shook her head, lounging on a large pile of pillows she'd arranged at her back.

"Oh yes." I nodded. "Though, to be honest, it didn't quite go as planned. Rather than actually kissing, we had a little accident and ended up smacking noses instead!" I covered my face with my hands, seeing the embarrassing moment so clearly it was as though it was happening all over again. "And before we could give it another try, a stranger interrupted us . . . and . . .well, the moment was lost." I shrugged. "But then later, by the fountain, he—"

"Stranger? What stranger?" Messalina bolted upright, her voice so edgy, face so alarmed, I immediately regretted having mentioned it.

"It's nothing," I told her, quick to wave it away, wanting to get back to my story—the second brief kiss Dacian had given me. "He left fairly quickly, it is nothing for you to worry about."

"But he must've wanted something—won't you tell me what that is?" She leaned toward me, her fingers reaching for my brow, pushing my hair away from my face.

"He was looking for someone named Riley." My gaze locked on hers. "Riley Bloom, I think he said."

"And what did you tell him?" She leaned closer, staring intently.

I sighed, longing to move past it, but one look at her face made it clear that was not going to happen unless we finished this first. "I didn't say anything." My gaze held fast to hers so she'd know it was true. "Dacian told him there was no one around by that name, that he had the wrong party, and should be on his way."

"And he did? He left?" Messalina asked, clearly on edge.

"He's gone. Not to worry, I doubt he'll return."

I looked away, bit down on my lip, struggling with the urge to take it all back, confess to my fib, tell her that he actually said just the opposite, leaving me to believe that he would return at some point. The war between the truth and the lie waging within me, until I saw the way her face softened, her shoulders slumped and relaxed, as she plucked an especially ripe-looking date from the tray and tossed it my way.

I plopped the squishy, puckered fruit into my mouth, closing my eyes to better savor its wonderful sweetness. The stranger's image blooming in my mind, unable to make sense of why I lied to my friend, why I clung to his promise of return—I only know that I did.

"So, what was the kiss like?" Messalina asked, returning to my favorite topic. "You are going to tell me, right? I want to hear every last detail!" She held a pillow to her chest, wrapped her arms around it and leaned toward me, urging, "So go ahead—what was it like? Was it as romantic as you hoped it would be? I mean, after all, it was your first kiss, right?"

I reached for my own pillow, took a long time fussing with it, getting it just right. Though that was all pretense—

buying the time that I needed in order to erase the memory of the green-eyed stranger and replace it with an image of Dacian. Then, once that was set, I was free to concentrate solely on the questions she'd asked.

I snuck a smile onto my face, plucked another date from the tray, and said, "The sky was sprinkled with stars—it couldn't have been more romantic." I closed my eyes, desperate to see it again. "There was even a shooting star—I'm so sorry you missed it."

"Did you make a wish?" Her voice so urgent my eyes snapped open just in time to see the serious look that crossed her face. "You should have," she said, nodding as she added, "you really, really should have. Most people wish for the moment to never end—or at least for the feeling to never end—and the wish is always granted, it never fails. They get to relive the experience again and again. Beautiful, isn't it?" She sighed and looked at me, and all I could do was nod in agreement.

16

The next morning, Messalina woke me by jiggling my arm and giggling in my ear as she said, "Wake up, sleepyhead—we've got a big day ahead!"

I ran a hand through my tangled mass of curls, lifted myself from the massive pile of pillows, and joined her at the trunk filled with what seemed to be an infinite amount of gorgeous, silky things she urged me to choose from.

"Go ahead! Pick something pretty!" She smiled brightly as she watched me riffle through it. Lifting a glossy stream of pink silk woven with intricate gold bits, only to have her snatch it away, and say, "Not that one." She fought for control of her face, tried to soften the edge, to not look as angry as her voice had already betrayed her to be. "I should've told you, I've already decided to wear pink today. And since I'm sure you'd prefer to stand out in front of Dacian, you'll need to choose another color."

I gazed longingly at the pink. Now that it was forbidden, I wanted it more than ever. Hoping to sway her when I said, "But we are like sisters, right?" I gazed at her from under my lashes. "Well, if we both wear pink then we can be even closer—almost like twins!"

The argument was a good one, sure to win her over, but Messalina wouldn't budge, wouldn't even pause to consider. She quickly dismissed it with an impatient wave of her hand, and reached for a dress that gleamed with the deepest shade of cobalt with traces of green woven in.

"*This*—this is the one, there is no doubt in my mind." She held the dress before me, urging me to agree, but my excitement was no match for hers, I was still mourning the loss of the pink. "With some sapphire jewelry, or maybe even lapis . . ." She pressed a finger to her chin as though seriously deciding between the two. "Well, either way, this one will serve you well, of that I've no doubt. It'll bring out your gorgeous blue eyes, to be sure. Dacian won't know what to do with himself when he sees you!"

Dacian.

The boy who kissed me.

The boy I was really beginning to like—wasn't I? Messalina seemed to think that was the case.

I fought to keep the facts straight—and yet, every time I tried to retrieve a memory of him, all I could see were swoopy brown bangs, odd clothes, bright green eyes, and a face so comforting yet unfamiliar I couldn't place it no matter how hard I tried.

I shook my head, desperate to rid myself of the thought. Messalina was staring, sensing a change in my mood, and not wanting to explain to her what I could barely explain to myself, I reached for the cobalt blue dress and slipped it right over my head. And once the complicated array of sashes and ties and jewelry and hair pins were all finally in place—once we were both shiny, and gorgeous, and elaborately dressed—Messalina linked her arm with mine, and said, "And now, let the games begin!"

The Colosseum was amazing, like nothing I'd ever seen before. My head forced to swivel from side to side in an effort to take it all in. Following Messalina into a private, shady box where all of Roman nobility sat, I turned to her and said, "Wow, look at all of these people! Is it always this crowded?"

"It is when Theocoles appears." She studied me carefully.

I nodded, vaguely familiar with the name. He was a champion. Went by some crazy nickname. Though I was quick to dismiss it, hardly interested in those particular details, I was more interested in finding Dacian.

"I hear Dacian's been asking about you all morning." Messalina smiled as though she'd just read my mind. "I hear he arrived early in anticipation of seeing you again." She leaned closer, giggled softly into my ear. "So let's not disappoint him, let's make sure everything is in place, shall we?" She stood before me, held me at arm's length as her gaze moved over me. Checking to make sure all was in place as she brushed a finger over my brow, saying, "Perfect. You are just perfect! I hope you enjoy the show, Aurelia—and believe me when I say that one never forgets their first time at the games!"

She pushed me toward Dacian, who reached for my hand and guided me to our seats where he immediately began chattering about the day's program.

The procession came first, quickly followed by games that were every bit as violent and gruesome as I assumed they would be. And yet, it wasn't long before I found myself sliding toward the edge of my seat, caught up in the same excitement as everyone around me. Cheering, and clapping, and stomping my feet—fully engrossed in the spectacle of horrific, unimaginable death, as one after another, the carcasses—both animal and human—began to pile up.

And when Theocoles took center stage, it became immediately clear why he was so revered. He was charismatic, magnetic, a bright and shining star in a sea of charmless brutes. The type of warrior one could easily pin all of their fantasies on.

The battle began, and I rooted along with the rest of them—greedy for more carnage, more slaying, more wounding, more bloodshed—consumed by an insatiable appetite for destruction that the previous battles had merely whetted. Torn between an eagerness to see Urbicus fall—torn to small, bloodied bits—and an eagerness for the show to go on, and on, and on so I could always feel so engaged.

My gazed riveted to the arena, eagerly following every blow, every leap, every swing of Theocoles' sword—until someone moved into the space right before me and blocked it from view.

"Excuse me!" I tapped him hard on the shoulder, wishing Dacian would step in and handle this for me, but his view was clear and his eyes were glued to the arena, not missing a thing. "Do you mind? I'm trying to watch the battle, much as you are, but unlike you, I can't see a thing, you are totally blocking me!"

The stranger turned, pushed his flop of hair away from his piercing green eyes, revealing himself to be the one from last night, only dressed far more appropriately in a blue-and-white toga that fell to his knees.

My mouth grew dry, my throat went all hot and tight, as my head swirled in a way I couldn't quite identify.

I mean, yes, he was cute.

Seriously cute.

Incredibly cute.

But no cuter than Dacian.

No cuter than my *new boyfriend* Dacian.

So why did I care? Why was I feeling this way? It just didn't make any sense.

"I didn't realize you were such a fan of the games, Riley. Usually you get completely grossed out by that much blood and gore. Usually you have a lot more respect for human life. I guess I misjudged you."

"My name isn't Riley," I snapped. It was the only thing I was sure of.

"Isn't it?" He looked at me, regarding me closely. "Well forgive me then, you remind me an awful lot of someone I once knew. Someone I'm *very* worried about. Someone I've been searching for."

"My name is Aurelia," I said, unable to break my gaze from his.

"Ah." He nodded. "And I am Bodhi." He reached for my hand, though as tempted as I was to take it, I held back. Dacian might be engaged in the games, too busy to notice, but I still wasn't sure if I should go through with it.

"You two together?" Bodhi asked, his eyes darting between Dacian and me.

I nodded, rubbed my lips together, and then nodded again.

"I won't keep you then," Bodhi said. "Still, I'm very pleased to meet you. I don't know many people in these parts, so it's nice to see a familiar face."

"Familiar?" I quirked my brow, unsure if he said that on purpose, or if it was an honest mistake.

But he was quick to dismiss it, laughing easily as he said, "Is that what I said? See, I guess you really do remind me of my friend, *Riley Bloom*. I meant to say *friendly*. It's nice to see a *friendly* face around here. This can be a tough crowd, in case you haven't noticed. Though you've seemed to fit in quite easily, haven't you?" His eyes squinted when he smiled, and he offered his hand once again.

I peered at Dacian, seeing he was still engrossed in the games. I reached forward and placed my hand in Bodhi's. Watching as he lowered his head, brushed his lips against the top of my hand, then lifted his eyes to meet mine, shooting me a saddened look that was soon interrupted by the roar of the crowd.

Theocoles had gone down, and the next thing I knew, the stranger, Bodhi, was racing toward the arena, racing toward Theocoles, as I turned to Dacian and said, "What is going on? What is he doing?"

"He's fallen," Dacian said, shaking his head in pity. "The Pillar of Doom has fallen."

I glanced from Dacian to the arena, saying, "No, I mean that guy, the stranger from last night—what is he doing down there?"

Dacian squinted, his brow creasing in confusion when he said, "I have no idea."

I jumped to my feet, pushed my way to the edge of the box where I watched as Bodhi knelt beside Theocoles, speaking urgently into his ear.

"I don't understand," I said, turning to Dacian, who'd made his way to me. "What are they doing down there? What's going on around here?"

My eyes darted wildly, wondering why no one else was bothered by what I could so clearly see.

"I think the heat and spectacle has gotten to us." Dacian laughed, grabbing my hand as he led me away. "It's a tragic turn of events, completely unexpected, to be sure. What do you say we find someplace quiet to sit, someplace where we can cool down. Night will fall soon, and once it does, we can search for our favorite constellations again." He looked at me with a face so open and hopeful it seemed impossible to resist.

And yet, I managed to pull away, managed to push my way back to the front of the box so I could peer into the arena. Surprised to find Messalina down there, following Theocoles, who followed his own dead body as it was dragged out of the arena and back behind those heavy iron gates. As Bodhi remained standing in the middle, his gaze locked on mine, telling me something I couldn't quite read no matter how hard I tried.

Our gaze broken when I heard a rush of laughter and noise, felt a light touch first on my arm, and then on my forehead, as I turned to find myself in the middle of a party with Messalina giggling beside me, as she introduced me to a super cute boy who went by the name of Dacian.

17

I needed air. Needed a break from the crowd and the noise. And, as cute as Dacian was, I needed a break from him too.

"Wait for me here?" I smiled, slipping a hand into my hair, making it fuller, poofier, knowing just from looking that he was so besotted with me, he'd do just about anything that I asked at that point.

"I'll come with you," he said, moving to follow.

Halted by the finality of my firmly stated, "No."

He stepped back. Shot me an injured look.

"Please," I said, resenting the need to lighten my tone but knowing it was necessary. He was nice, he was cute, there was no need to upset him. "I just need a moment alone. I'll be back before you know it, I promise."

He nodded reluctantly, but it was enough to release me. And though I was tempted to run, I forced myself to walk as I wound my way through the maze of party guests and found my way out the door.

I leaned against the balcony, leaned my head back, and lost myself in the night, hoping the cool air might work a bit of magic by finding a way to cure my confusion—all the strange feelings nagging inside.

I had everything a girl could want, and yet, something felt lacking, missing, though I had no idea what.

I gazed up at the sky, my eyes searching for constellations, easily finding Cassiopeia, Draco, but stumbling when it came to Andromeda.

"Andromeda is right there."

I stiffened, expecting to find Dacian, and surprised to find a stranger instead.

"How'd you know I was looking for Andromeda?" My eyes moved over him, taking in a swoop of brown hair, bright green eyes, and an odd green object he clenched in his teeth.

"Because Andromeda is your favorite." He smiled, taking another step toward me.

"And how would you know that?" I asked, my voice more than a little bit testy.

"Good question." He nodded, pretending to think. "How would I know that?" He moved until he stood right beside me, whispering, "*Think*, Riley. Just close your eyes, block all this out, and think as hard as you can. How would I know that? Try to remember if you can."

"I—I don't know . . ." I looked all around, suddenly regretting my decision to be out on my own. "And why do you call me Riley?"

"Because that's your name."

"My name is Aurelia," I said, though there was no mistaking the doubt creeping into my voice.

"Is it?" He cocked his head, slipped the green object across his front teeth, and stared at me intently.

"Listen, I don't know what you . . ." The words died on my tongue as a beautiful, yellow haired animal ran up beside me, wagging a fluffy tail with excitement, and happily licking my fingers. "What is it?" I said, unsure if I should be flattered by the beast's attention, or completely grossed out by the way it slobbered all over me.

"That's Buttercup. He's your dog, and he's very happy to see you. You've been gone a long time, Riley. Too long. We've both been very worried about you."

"Worried? About me? Why would you be worried about me?"

"Because I . . ." The stranger paused, forced himself to look away for a moment before he returned to me and started again. "Because it's *my job* to worry about you."

"Your *job*? What are you, like my guardian angel or

something?" I laughed at the thought.

"I'm your guide. Not quite the same thing, though they do share certain similarities."

"Do you have any idea how crazy this sounds?" I shook my head, telling myself I should leave, find my way back into the party, and to do it quickly.

But somehow I couldn't.

Somehow I just remained right there in place.

"Just because something sounds crazy doesn't make it any less true." He ducked his head, gazed up at me through a thick row of lashes. "Sometimes you just have to take a leap of faith, tune out what you see before you, what other people tell you, and focus on what you know deep down inside your own heart."

I gazed between the stranger and the beast, then started to turn away, stopped by the sound of his voice when he said, "You're quite a vision, Riley. Truly."

My breath hitched, as chills ran over my flesh.

"I can see why you've chosen to stay. The first moment I saw you like this, you took my breath away." He shook his head, ran a nervous hand over his chin. "And now that I've said that, I can only hope that when I find a way to break you out of here, you will not remember it."

I twisted the rings on my hands, unable to remove my gaze from his. Carefully committing his words to memory, sensing they were far more meaningful than they first seemed—sure that I'd once longed to hear them—though I had no idea who he was.

Or did I?

I could no longer be sure.

"You know it's not real, right?" His voice was gentle, his eyes filled with kindness. "You know you have to accept that—you have to find your way out. You can have all this and more. In fact, you are well on your way. You just have to be patient, Riley. It will come. I promise you that. You can have everything you want in the Here & Now—you don't have to be here."

That tingly feeling his words had brought vanished just as quickly. He was wrong. I *did* need to be here. Everything I was depended on it. He had no idea what he was talking about.

"Listen," I said, my gaze leveled on his, my voice full of venom, "I don't know who you think you are, but—"

"My name is Bodhi." He nodded. Then pointing at the beast he said, "I am your guide, Buttercup is your dog, and you are *not* Aurelia, you are Riley. A twelve-year-old Soul Catcher who resides in the Here & Now. You are visiting Rome on assignment. You are meant to find a gladiator named Theocoles and convince him to cross over. You are *not* from this time. This is *not* your home. These people are *not* your friends. And, that is *not* how you look in real life. You are dead. And it's time you find your way out of here and get on with your afterlife."

Dead?

Dead!

I shut my eyes tightly, fought back the surge of crystalline tears that threatened to pour down my cheeks. Gathering my skirts and shaking my head, I looked at him once more and said, "No! *No.*" Though my voice sounded tired, broken, bearing not a single trace of conviction. "No way. You need to leave. You need to leave *now*—and you need to take your . . ." I swallowed, regretting the words before they were out. But I had no choice. I was desperate to hang onto Aurelia, and the longer they stayed, the more impossible that would be. "You need to take your smelly beast with you before I scream for help and have you both dragged away."

The beast looked at me, its eyes slanting, tail sinking low between his legs, the moment he heard me call him *smelly*. And though the sight saddened me, I didn't apologize. I needed to be rid of them, find my way back inside, my new life as Aurelia depended on it.

"Riley, please—"

Bodhi, the stranger who claimed to be my guide, reached for me, touched me, his fingers circling my wrist, inviting me to follow—and I almost caved—I almost did, until Messalina appeared out of nowhere, with Dacian standing beside her.

"Is there a problem?" Her gaze narrowed in anger.

I yanked free of Bodhi's grip, wiped the warm place on my arm where his fingers had been as though I couldn't wait to erase every last trace of him.

"Everything's fine," I said, stepping forward to take Dacian's side. "He's found his way to the wrong party, mistaken me for someone else, but now that he knows the truth, now that he knows I'm *not* the girl he's searching for, he and his beast will move on. Won't you?"

I narrowed my gaze on Bodhi's, holding it for as long as I could. My heart plummeting, a sick feeling invading me, fighting the urge to run after them, when he turned and left, dragging the dog along with him.

Messalina, satisfied with their departure, left me in Dacian's care the moment they were gone. The two of us gazing into the vast night sky, pointing to our favorite constellations—including the one he'd named just for me. And it wasn't long after that, when he closed his eyes, leaned forward, and kissed me.

18

When Theocoles fell, the entire Colosseum went silent. I glanced at Dacian, seeing his face go slack, his mouth hang wide, then I glanced at Messalina behind me, noting how she was the only one among us unable to watch.

When Theocoles rolled over and his eyes searched for Messalina's, the crowd was quick to recover—quick to turn on him and chant, "Kill!"

And when Urbicus lifted his sword, waiting for the emperor's consent—when Messalina had already fled, unable to watch her lover's slaughter yet again—when a stranger moved before me and fought to meet my gaze—I dropped Dacian's hand and leaped, jumped, and fought my way to the center of the arena—possessed by a drive and a strength I didn't know I possessed.

"*Theocoles!*" I called, knowing I had to move fast as there was no time for subtlety, no time to waste. "Theocoles—stop!"

I dropped to my knees, knelt right beside him, registering the shocked look on his face as he took in the gruesome state of his sad, headless corpse.

Repeating all the same words I'd said before—but just like before I was unable to get through to him—he resisted me at every turn.

"I will win their favor—they will worship me once more!" He shouted, rising to his feet, reaching for the helmet he sunk onto his head. "I will not be forgotten! I will be remembered! I will gain their admiration again!"

He retrieved his sword, picked up his shield, and I was just about to address him again, when Messalina sprang up behind me and said, "You're much tougher than you look." Her gaze burned on mine as she made her approach. "You're surprisingly resilient for a *young* girl your age." She stood before me, her words pointed, chosen carefully, and I knew without looking that the magic was gone.

I was no longer gorgeous, teenaged Aurelia—I was back to being skinny, scrawny, little Riley Bloom. Drowning in a pool of silky blue fabric that hung in unflattering droops, as Messalina shook her head, tsking in pity as her tongue clicked the roof of her mouth.

"What would Dacian say?" she wondered aloud.

Dacian.

I sighed, sure that he wouldn't say much of anything if

he saw me like this. Heck, he wouldn't even recognize me in my current state—definitely wouldn't cross rooms just to meet me—much less name constellations after me—never mind attempt to hold my hand and kiss me.

But then a new thought occurred. Something so horrifying I hesitated to voice it.

Forcing the words from my mouth when I said, "I don't know Messalina, what *would* Dacian say?" I brought my finger to my chin, screwed my lips to the side as though deeply contemplating. "My guess is he would say whatever you make him say, since, after all, he is your creation, isn't he? As soulless as the guests at your never-ending party, as soulless as the Roman nobles who crowd your uncle's box." I stared hard at her, wanting her to know that while it might hurt to realize my boyfriend had been fake, I refused to be devastated. "As soulless as everyone here, but you, and me, and of course, Theocoles."

"Is that what you think?" she asked, her voice low and soft.

I shrugged. I mean, I wasn't absolutely sure of it, I had no real proof, but it seemed like a pretty good theory.

"I miss our friendship," she said, moving right past that, refusing to either confirm or deny. "You and I were such great friends, weren't we?" She smiled slowly as though lost in the memory. "Believe me when I say that it was truly the most fun I've had in a very long time. There is nothing you can say that will make me think otherwise."

"You *enchanted* me!" I shook my head, hardly believing what she'd just said. "You had me under your spell. And every time I'd start to find my way out—you brushed your hand across my forehead and put me under again!"

"Yeah? So?" She shrugged. "Do you mean to tell me you didn't enjoy yourself?"

I mashed my lips together, buried my hands in the folds of my skirt, knowing that I had. I'd enjoyed myself far more than I cared to admit. Enjoyed myself so much, I'd chosen to stay, to pretend, even after Bodhi and Buttercup had managed to wake me.

Messalina's world was alluring, tempting—it allowed me to live my own fairy tale—the kind of life I'd always dreamed of with fancy parties, pretty dresses, and a really cute prince by my side. If I'd stayed under her spell, I'd be happy for a very long time, perhaps even eternity. I'd live the same day over and over again, sure, but it's not like I'd know the difference.

But while her world was soft and comfortable, offering everything I could ever want, it all came too easy. There was something to be said for patience and hard work.

There was something to be said for realizing your dream the old-fashioned way, by actually earning it.

"It doesn't have to end, you know?" She smiled, lifted her hand. "You're the little sister I always wanted, we can return to that easily, just say the word and it's done."

My bangs lay limp against my forehead, while the bodice of my dress sagged in the most embarrassing way—providing two very good reasons to give my consent, along with a whole heap of others that lined up behind it. All I had to do was allow her to brush her finger across my brow and I could dissolve into bliss. Though as tempting as it was, still I said, "No." My face stern, eyes narrowed, so she'd know that I meant it. "Besides, I already have a sister, and someday, we'll be together again. But for now, I'm content with the memories." *Memories and occasional visits to the Viewing Room, not to mention Dreamland.* I nodded toward Theocoles, then returned my gaze to hers. "You know I have a job to do. You know I'm here to get through to him—to help him move on."

"And you know that I can't let you do that," she said, her face sincere with regret.

"Then it seems we've reached a stalemate," I said, watching as she turned away from me in favor of him.

Returning to a scene that had first taken places handfuls of centuries earlier. The one where Theocoles stared in bewilderment when he followed his own dead body as it was dragged from the arena.

My voice calling after her as I said, "It doesn't end here! I will not give up until I've finished what I came for!"

The words falling on deaf ears as the gladiator and his girlfriend disappeared behind the big iron gates.

19

"Riley!" Bodhi called out to me, reached for me, but I just kept going, swerving right past him, right past poor whining Buttercup as I found my way out of the Colosseum and onto the street.

"You were great back there," Bodhi said, running to keep up with me. "Really, as your guide I have to say I was truly impressed."

I slumped down onto a big stone slab and buried my face in my hands, mumbling, "Yeah? Well, you shouldn't be. The whole thing's been nothing but a big, fat, colossal fail since the moment I got here."

"How do you figure?" Bodhi sat beside me, as Buttercup tried to sniff and lick at my fingers but I pushed him away.

"How do *you* figure?" I asked, knowing I was acting like a brat, but unable to voice the real reason behind it.

It was the way Bodhi had looked at me when I was

Aurelia—versus the way he looked at me now. The two were polar opposites, worlds apart, as different as me and, well, as different as me and Aurelia were.

"You found your way out," Bodhi said. "You're the first Soul Catcher to accomplish such a thing."

"I didn't accomplish anything," I told him. "I found my way out because of you, and Buttercup. Your showing up while I was out on the balcony triggered something in me, though I did my best to fight it so I could continue to live as Aurelia." I lifted my head, and searched for his eyes. "And, for the record, I heard everything you said. I remember *all* of it." I shot him a pointed look, wondering if he understood what I was referring to—the bit when he confessed that I, or rather me masquerading as Aurelia, took his breath away. I shook my head and groaned, waved my hand before me, wishing I could erase what I'd just said. There was no point in going on about it. "The only reason I didn't let on is because I didn't exactly want to be out. Before I agreed to enter her world, I made her promise not to trap me. But, once she did, I didn't fight too hard to get out. Messalina gave me everything I ever wanted and more. And, at that moment anyway, the Here & Now just couldn't compete with the fairy tale life she'd created for me."

"So, what changed your mind?" he asked, his voice gentle but curious.

I started to say, "*You*."

Started to say that the thought of being around him, even stuck as little Riley Bloom, the girl he'd never take seriously, was what did it—but I just couldn't get to the words.

So instead, I swallowed hard and said, "Buttercup." I patted my lap, invited my big lug of a dog to jump up. Grasping him tightly to a chest that was once again sunken, I said, "I missed Buttercup." And then I buried my face in his fur, mumbling my apologies into his ear. "I'm sorry for calling you smelly, because you're not—or at least not in a bad way, not in the way of the *ludus*. You smell like fresh air and sunshine and . . ." I scrunched my nose deep into his neck. "And strawberries! Have you been rolling in a field of strawberries?" I peered into his big brown eyes, hoping to find a hint of forgiveness. And when he barked in excitement, when he licked my face and left a pool of slobber all over my cheeks, I knew we were good once again.

"So what now?" Bodhi asked, his question so broad I wasn't sure if he meant: *What now after the weird thing we experienced?*

Or more like: *What do we do now—what's the strategy for getting what we came for?*

Choosing to stick with the least uncomfortable of the two, I gazed down at my dress, tightened the braided gold sash around my waist, and said, "Well, I'm pretty sure we can find Messalina and Theocoles in either one of two places—at the party, or the games. From what I can tell, they just relive the same two experiences over and over again."

20

I was really hoping we'd find them at the games since I'd had enough of that whole party scene. And, in all honesty, I was hoping to avoid Dacian as well.

Partly due to vanity—I couldn't bear the thought of him seeing me as myself—my *real* self as opposed to my *future* self. And partly because I was pretty sure he wasn't real anyway. I was pretty sure he was nothing more than a manifestation Messalina had made to better distract me. The fact that she refused to either confirm or deny it, the fact that she just slid around the question, only proved it.

But, as luck would have it, when we arrived the party was in full swing, Messalina was already down in the *ludus*, and there was no sign of Dacian, which only confirmed my suspicion. Dacian was a fake. Otherwise, he would've been there, caught up in the same, lame routine. But since I was no longer a participant, Messalina was free to delete

him from the guest list. And yet, even though I already suspected, I'm not gonna lie, it still hurt like heck.

Hurt in a way that surprised me.

My fairy-tale romance was not only completely superficial—not only based on a lie—but, in actuality, it didn't
even exist.

My first real kiss wasn't real at all—it had come from a
soulless aberration disguised as Prince Charming. And I'd
wanted so badly to believe it was true that I bought right
into the illusion Messalina had made.

How's that for pathetic?

We made our way down the stairs, pushing through
the crowd of raging gladiator ghosts, until we came to
the second-to-last cell, and I motioned for Bodhi to peek
through the small square opening at the top, to take in the
scene I knew all too well.

"Wow, he really is stuck," Bodhi whispered, turning
away from the door and glancing at me.

I stared at him, suddenly struck by something I hadn't
noticed before.

"What?" Bodhi's brows drew together as Buttercup tilted
his head and stared at me inquisitively.

"Say it again," I urged. "Repeat exactly what you just said,
in the exact same tone of voice."

He looked at me like I'd lost it, though he was quick

to go along, whispering, "Wow, he really is stuck." Then staring at me, waiting for the big reveal.

"That's it!" I pulled him away from the door, and motioned for Buttercup to run alongside me, glancing over my shoulder to say, "Listen, when we get to the top of the stairs we'll find ourselves in the Colosseum. I don't know how it happens, I just know that it's always happened that way in the past, so I'm sure it'll happen again. So just follow my lead, okay?"

Bodhi nodded, his trust in me complete. And as I tore up the stairs and found my way to the landing that's when I learned that I really was in Messalina's world—and the rules of the game could change in an instant.

21

I stared in confusion, having no idea how this could've happened. We weren't at the games, weren't anywhere near the Colosseum from what I could tell. The only thing I knew for sure is that Messalina was messing with me. If she couldn't keep me under her spell, then she'd keep me trapped in her maze.

Bodhi cocked his head, looking to me for direction. Figuring since I'd spent so much time here I must know the way, and at that moment, I suddenly understood his job better—the huge responsibility involved in guiding others. I also understood how horrible it must've been for him to be stuck as my guide, when I tended to fight him every step of the way, ensuring his job was anything but easy.

Surely being stuck in a maze of empty white rooms that all looked the same, feeling about as lost as it gets as my dog and my guide waited for me to lead them to escape, was nothing more than the payback I so richly deserved. Though payback or not, I had no choice but to overcome it, to do whatever it took to find our way out.

I forced myself to go quiet and still, on the lookout for any signs that might help, and it wasn't long before I heard a burst of noise drifting from a place nearby, motioning for Bodhi and Buttercup to follow alongside me. We crept down a series of corridors, through a succession of identical rooms, progressing toward the sound of laughter, music, and chatter that seemed to grow louder and louder with each passing step, though no matter how far we went, we couldn't locate the source, never got any closer than when we began.

I stopped, coming to such a quick and sudden halt that Bodhi bumped right into me, and Buttercup into him—the chain reaction knocking me off balance, forcing me to reach toward the wall to steady myself.

"Sorry," Bodhi whispered, starting to say something more when I raised my finger to my lips, shooting him and Buttercup a warning of silence.

Listen, I thought, knowing he could hear it as clearly as any words I might speak. *Listen as hard as you can*.

Bodhi leaned forward as Buttercup mimicked by cocking an ear and holding the pose for a moment before turning to me in confusion.

I don't hear anything—or at least anything that stands out from the laughter and chatter. Bodhi looked at me, face thoroughly confused.

I nodded. Finally getting the full picture of what I'd only glimpsed before. "Instead of moving **toward** the noise, we should've been moving *away* from it."

Bodhi looked in both directions before returning to me.

"The noise is a distraction. It's keeping us from our goal. Just like it's keeping Theocoles from his destiny."

Bodhi sighed, shrugged, clearly having no idea what I meant, but eager to get on with it, he jabbed a thumb over his shoulder and said, "So, we go that way instead?"

I nodded. "Head into the silence." I slipped in front of him, taking the lead. "Head to the place where the noise becomes no more than a whisper. That's where we'll find him—and that's where we'll need to lead him as well."

22

We headed back through the maze, back down the stairs, and back toward the *ludus*, moving away from the noise Messalina had manifested to bait us, until reaching the long row of cells where I stopped, listened intently, and hearing the roar of the crowd, moved in the direction it came from.

"Wait—I thought we wanted to move *away* from the noise?" Bodhi said, keeping pace beside me.

"We did." I nodded, quickening my pace.

"But now we're moving toward it—again."

"Yep." I navigated a series of turns, trying not to overthink it—that would only lead to doubt and confusion. If I wanted to end this, I had to commit to my instincts.

"I don't get it," Bodhi said, his voice sounding discouraged, as though he was ready to move in and take charge.

"You may not get it now, but you will, I promise. You have to trust me."

I looked at him, taking in the swoop of his hair, and his thick fringe of lashes, then I looked away just as quickly. Unsure why I felt such a sudden surge of loss when we were getting along better than ever, but there was no doubt things had changed. Changed in a way that was much bigger than either of us probably realized. Whether it was good change or bad change remained to be seen—all I knew for sure is that all change stems from a loss of something that came before.

"The party noise was intended to distract us, to lead us toward something that didn't exist," I told him. "Messalina manifested it. There are no party guests—she just makes it appear that way. The only thing that's real is what happens between her and Theocoles."

"What about those other Soul Catchers? Did you run into any of them? They're still out here, disguised as party guests, gladiators, house slaves, and who knows what else?"

I shrugged. I had no way of knowing what happened to them, and I hated to say it, but it really was none of my concern. I'd been warned about making up my own assignments, it was a lesson I'd learned the hard way, but at least I can say that I truly did learn it. Which meant that the fate of anyone other than Theocoles was none of my business. The Council was in charge, not me.

"We'll deal with that later." I glanced over my shoulder. "But for now, all you need to know is that wherever you hear the roar of the crowd, that's where you'll find Theocoles. It's what he lived for, what he inadvertently died for—and it's the one thing he refuses to give up."

We turned another corner and I couldn't help but smile in triumph when the light hit my eyes so hard I was forced to squint and shield my face with my hand.

"The Colosseum," Bodhi said, as poor Buttercup sniffed the air and gazed around anxiously, sensing the lingering agony of all the poor animals that came here before him only to die a terrible death. "The *ludus* had a passageway that led right to it, I guess I'd forgotten that."

We stood beside the big iron gates, watching the last few minutes of the fight—the remaining moments right before Theocoles died—before the crowd scorned him, turned on him, demanded he pay for what they perceived as an act of cowardice. And I looked at Bodhi, said, "Please, wait here— please, just let me handle this." Then without another word, I sped toward the arena. Knowing Messalina never arrived until later, but that she would arrive, of that I'd no doubt. It was a dance they'd repeated too many times, and Messalina was just as caught up in it as he was.

She was also, apparently, on to me, because I'd barely made my way across the sand when she appeared right before me, and said, "If you don't want to stay and enjoy the party, then perhaps you should leave. I've tried to be a good hostess. I've tried to provide you with everything your heart desires. But it doesn't seem to be enough for you. You want more. You want something I can never allow you to have. You can't fight me, Riley, and neither can your friends." She motioned toward the place where Buttercup and Bodhi waited. "So perhaps it's time we say our goodbyes."

"I thought you loved him?" I moved toward her. "I thought you wanted to be with him? I thought you were planning a future together?" I looked at her, her eyes shining brightly as she stood before me, haughty, regal—the queen of her own tragic fairy tale.

"I do," she said quietly. "And I will have all of that, you will see. But when it does happen, it will be because of *me*. Theocoles will awaken because of me. *Me*, Riley, *not* you! My love will pull him through. One day he will look at me again, in real time, not in some past-life mirage. One day he will see the real me standing before him, and that will be enough. He'll remember the love that we shared and it will shake him from the past. But it has to come from *me*, Riley. Why can't you understand that? Why can't you all just let us be?"

My jaw dropped in astonishment as a new understanding began to take shape. "You think you're to blame." My eyes met hers, and I knew it was true by the way she flinched in response. "You think he blames you for what happened to him."

"What? And you see it differently?" She shot me a pitying look. "He was put to his death because he rolled over to look at *me*! He lost the battle—of that there's no doubt—but he was the crowd favorite—surely they would've taken mercy—surely they would've chanted *live* instead of *kill* if he hadn't done what he did. How were they to know his eyes went in search of me? No one knew about us—no one *could* know about us—my uncle would've never allowed it! Would've interfered and done whatever it took to stop it. But, as fate would have it, my uncle got just as he would've wished. I was standing beside him, when Theocoles' eyes met mine, and that's when my uncle confirmed what he'd already begun to suspect. But did he whisper in the emperor's ear? Did he find a way to intervene? No. He allowed it to happen. And, when it was done, he turned to me and said, 'It is for the best. Someday you will thank me.'"

She shook her head, her gaze bearing the loss as though it were fresh. "So make no mistake, Riley, Theocoles *does* blame me. I've been here for thousands of years and not once have I broken through to him. He refuses to see me unless it's a scene we relive from the past. It's the crowd he adores. It's a love I cannot compete with—it's a fate I've come to accept. Though my love for him burns brighter than ever, in all of these years it has not dimmed in the slightest. If anything, it's just made me more determined. So please, please leave us to do what we do. Check back in another hundred years if you must, but for now, leave us be until then."

"You're willing to wait it out for another century?"

She nodded.

"Another hundred years of the same, lame routine?"

"It may be all the same—but it's certainly not lame. I get to be near him—and that's all that matters to me."

I looked at her, this beautiful, charming ghost I once confused as my friend. And despite how evil I once thought she was, I couldn't help but feel sorry for her. She was misguided, there was no getting around it, but everything she did, was done out of love.

I gazed down at the sand, caught in a quandary I hadn't expected. There was no way I'd leave her be for another hundred years, that was out of the question. Especially now that I knew exactly how to awaken Theocoles from the past—knew exactly how to get through to him. A discovery that would surely place me in the Soul Catcher Hall of Fame—if there were such a thing—a discovery that all the other Soul Catchers would talk about in awe for years to come. They might even name a holiday after me in order to celebrate what was sure to be a monumental victory.

Thing was, it didn't really have to be *me* who did it. I could just as easily tell Messalina the secret and provide her the script. After all, she'd spent the last several centuries just waiting for this moment—and I just wasn't sure I could steal it from her—no matter how much glory it would mean for me.

I buried my big toe deep into the sand, knowing it would be just as easy to push right past her and claim center stage.

Easy, but not necessarily right.

And definitely not at all kind.

Then I heaved a great sigh, looked up at her, and said, "While there's no way I'm leaving you here for the next hundred years—I will leave you this: If you want to get through to Theocoles, you need to learn how to whisper . . ."

23

"I don't get it." She glanced between the gladiator and me, face full of judgment and scorn. "How could that possibly work? He only responds to the roar of the crowd—and as far as he's concerned the louder the better. Why would he pay attention to something he can't even hear? Something sure to be drowned out by the noise?"

"Because sometimes there's more worth in silence than noise," I said, desperate for her to understand what I'd just come to learn for myself. "Sometimes everything you need to know is contained in that small quiet space. Sometimes we get so caught up in distraction and noise and seeking other people's approval we forget the quiet seed of truth that lives in our hearts. But just because we fail to tune in to it, doesn't mean it's not there. Theocoles loves you. I know, because I saw you together in his cell—I saw the look he gave you after he fell in the arena—"

"Yeah, and it's because of that look that he refuses to look at me now." She shook her head, folded her arms across her chest. "I'm sorry, Riley, I know you're only trying to help, which is pretty amazing after all that I've put you through, but I just don't see the point in—"

"I didn't see the point in trying on the blue dress the day we first met. I didn't see the point in manifesting a new and improved version of me. But in the end, it worked, and no matter how things turned out, for a while anyway, the results made me happy." I nodded, wanting her to realize the truth behind my words, but she was quick to dismiss it.

"That was different, that was an outcome within my control." She shrugged, looked away.

"Was it?" I quirked a brow, refused to give up. "I mean, I'm the one who came up with the vision of how I wanted to look—not you. So didn't I play some part in the way things turned out?"

She looked at me, a new understanding beginning to dawn on her face.

"Try it," I urged. "What can it hurt to try when you have nothing left to lose?"

She nodded, ran her hands over the front of her gorgeous pink gown, fussed with her curls, adjusted her necklace and rings, and approached him. Standing beside him as he stared at his corpse, mumbling in confusion, where she proceeded to do the exact opposite of what I'd just counseled.

Instead of approaching him gently, quietly, she turned toward the crowd, threw her head back, opened her arms wide, and sent them into a state of uncontrolled frenzy—the stadium rumbling with the sound of: *Theocoles! Theocoles! Long live Theocoles, the Pillar of Doom!*

The chorus repeating again and again as Theocoles stopped, alerted to their cry of noisy admiration, he gazed around wildly, threw his head back, spread his arms wide, and soaked it all in.

"What's she doing?" Bodhi asked, having come up beside me.

I shook my head in reply. Disappointed didn't even begin to describe how I felt.

"But, more importantly, what are *you* doing?" he said, staring intently.

I looked at him, unsure what he meant.

"Giving away your Soul Catch to a ghost who tricked you?" He frowned. "The Riley Bloom I know would never do such a thing. She wouldn't even consider giving up the glory."

Oh, that.

I nodded, shrugged, unsure just how to explain it other than to say, "I guess it just seemed like the right thing to do. You know, the kind, mature thing to do. But, maybe I misjudged her."

I closed my eyes to better listen to the lecture that played in my head. The one that chided me for my foolishness—that scolded me for trusting someone who'd tricked me numerous times already. But just as that internal dialogue began to take hold, a new thought moved in and stopped it cold.

What I was doing was the same thing Theocoles had done for a pile of centuries. I was tuning in to my hurt pride, my bruised ego, my tarnished self-image, my wounded vanity—I was so focused on the lecture, I ignored the quiet truth that lived deep inside. And once I'd silenced the noise in my head, I realized the noise in the arena had vanished as well.

Messalina had taken my advice after all.

Theocoles staggered, floundered his way across the sand, searching for his helmet, his sword, and his shield—ready to enter into his tireless routine yet again.

But just as he reached for them, Messalina made them each vanish—one by one—until he spun in confusion, unsure what to do.

"I know you prefer to hear them," she whispered, gesturing toward the stadium. She filled the stands briefly with a crowd that clapped and cheered, noting the way Theocoles' eyes lit up at the sight of it, the sound of it, and how quickly they extinguished the moment she took it away. "But I've indulged you for too long, and now I'm hoping you'll listen to me instead of them."

He moved right past her, knocking into her, completely unaware of her, causing her to look my way, her face broken, longing for encouragement, approval, which I happily gave.

"I've been trying to reach you for so long now," she said. "I have so much to tell you. There are so many things you used to care about—so many goals you used to work toward—and though it seems you have forgotten them, that you've turned your back and ceased caring about them—I still want you to know that just after you died, I saw that your brother was freed. I told you I would provide the money, I told you that you didn't have to fight for it, and I kept my promise. I had him released from the mines, and I'm happy to say that because of it, Lucius was able to live a long and fulfilling life. I also had a monument built in your honor. It was a bust of your face, with your name on a plaque just underneath so that no one would ever forget who you were, or that you were once the reigning champion of the Colos-seum. It stood for a very long time, hundreds of years, to be sure. It stood just outside of these walls. Though unfortu-nately it was knocked down not long after the fall. Yes, the empire has fallen." She smiled. "So much has changed—some of Rome is not at all recognizable—and some is much like you left it. Not that you got to see much outside of the *ludus*—but the point is, you are no longer stuck here. Or at least you don't have to be. The choice is yours. But if you choose to stay here, well, you will stay here alone." She glanced over her shoulder, meeting my gaze as she said, "I'm tired of this same, lame routine. I'm sorry that you've never seen fit to forgive me. But maybe it's time I forgive myself. Maybe it's time for me to move on to what's next."

She moved toward him, grabbed hold of his shoulders and stared hard into his face, repeating the words I'd fed her just moments before. "I wish you would learn to tune out the roar of the crowd, and instead, listen to the whisper of truth that lives in your heart."

He tried to move away, tried to move past her, still on a quest for his missing sword, but Messalina held firm, her hands grasping his arms as she finished the script I'd given to her. "Your heart always knows what's important. It always knows how to guide you. It's pure, and trustworthy—though it will never shout to be heard. It will never speak above a whisper. But if you learn how to heed it, how to hear it, you will never feel lost in the world."

He pushed her aside, lurched forward, continued to stagger across the sand, as I sagged in frustration, knowing she did the best that she could, that I couldn't have done any better. I guess this was one Soul Catch neither one of us could cross over.

I started to turn, started to motion to Bodhi to leave. My

feelings conflicted, knowing I'd done all I could, though that didn't make it any easier. Defeat was something I did not handle well.

Reminded of the words Bodhi said before I'd even started this journey, some old Gandhi quote, "Full effort is full victory." And though its meaning was clear, I was hardly in the mood to celebrate any effort that didn't end in victory, it's just how I was.

I met Bodhi's eyes, trying not to feel ashamed in front of my guide, totally missing the way he gestured, pointed behind me, until he said, "Look."

I turned to see Theocoles, brow scrunched in confusion, as he watched Messalina cross the arena.

The Colosseum so quiet you could hear a butterfly take flight, broken by Theocoles' fervent cry, "*Messalina!*"

She stopped, her eyes wide, as she spun on her heel to face him. Her body still, face cautiously hopeful, as though she couldn't quite believe that the moment she'd been waiting for had finally come to fruition.

"Messalina—where am I?" He gazed around in confusion. "Where have they gone?" He motioned toward a stadium, once filled to capacity, but now empty.

"Home," she said, her voice like a sigh. "They left the Colosseum a very long time ago. We're the only ones left. Well, the only original ones anyway."

"And Lucius? He is free, it is true what you said?"

She nodded, approaching him until she stood just inches away, saying, "Yes."

"And I—I am free as well?"

She closed her eyes, savoring his question, and opening them again when she said, "Yes. Finally. After all of these centuries, you are now free. That is, if you choose to be. In the end, it's up to you."

"And our future?"

She smiled, eye shining with hope and a surge of crystalline tears. "Ours to seize whenever we're ready."

He reached toward her, big, brutal hands cupping her cheeks with a tenderness I would've never imagined. Gazing upon her as though she was a precious mirage he feared would soon fade.

"And your uncle—he approves of our union, then?" His thumbs smoothed over her skin, his eyes fixed on hers as though no time had passed, as though he'd merely woken from a brief nap.

"No." She shook her head, her fingers reaching up to meet his. "I'm afraid, he never came around to the idea. Though he's hardly an issue anymore. The only thing that can stop us from moving forward, is *you*."

"Me?" He stepped back, gazed around in confusion again, but only for a moment before the weight of his reality hit him. "Then it truly is over. I am no longer enslaved by your uncle—no longer enslaved by . . . *them*." He gestured toward the empty stands. "And all of this—" He gazed down at his feet, kicked at the pile of rose petals he once held so dear, suddenly realizing he'd traded a love that'd never once faltered, for one that was as fickle as the wind.

"I should hope not," she said. "But in the end, that is also up to you."

"Then what are we waiting for?" he asked, moving toward her with purpose.

"We wait for nothing," she said, smiling as she melted into his arms.

24

Theocoles walked alongside me as Messalina hung back with Bodhi and Buttercup. An arrangement I didn't quite expect, but then again nothing was going as planned.

Even though I knew he had a soft side (after all, I'd seen it firsthand when I watched him in the *ludus* with Messalina), it was still kind of surprising to see how gentle he was. I mean, for a big, hulking, mass of a guy—one who definitely lived up to his nickname, Pillar of Doom, he spoke to me with such kindness, I had no doubt that the person I saw in the arena was more like a role he'd taken on in order to survive—a role that got away from him, sure—but it wasn't who he really was deep down inside.

And while I was more than ready to make the shimmering golden veil right then and there, and send him directly from the arena to the bridge, Theocoles had been pent up in the *ludus* and Colosseum for so long, he wanted to see what had become of Rome before he moved on.

He wanted to see the real Rome—the modern Rome—the one with flushing toilets and running water.

Though as much as I preferred the new and improved, less barbaric version, Theocoles wasn't quite so impressed.

"So, what do you think?" I asked, after having made a pretty good tour of the place.

He looked at me, shaking his head when he said, "This is how people dress?" He glanced around again, face dropping into a frown when he added, "I can hardly tell the women from the men!"

I rolled my eyes, I couldn't help but take that personally since I'd ditched the baggy blue gown the first chance I got, exchanging it for jeans, a (super cute) tee, and ballet flats. And with my hair scraped into a ponytail, with my body back to its former stick-figure self, well, the statement felt like it was directed at me. Not to mention the fact that it came from a man who'd spent his entire life wearing a dress!

I shot him an injured look, saying, "Well, get used to it. Times have changed. Besides, not everyone can be as amazing as Messalina. Some of us are a little less fortunate in the girly department."

"Messalina truly *is* the fairest of them all," he said, gazing back at her to confirm it. Then returning to me, he added, "And you, Miss Riley Bloom, should not underestimate yourself—you may be young yet, but you show great promise." He leaned down, flicked my ponytail, and sent it swinging back and forth, grinning at me in a way that made his topaz eyes twinkle and my throat go all tight and hot. The guy just oozed charm and charisma, he couldn't help it, he was magnetic in every possible way.

"So, this is pretty much it," I said, eager to cross him over and move on. "Old stuff, new stuff, cars, scooters, people, busy-busy-busy—seen enough?" We'd come full circle again and the Colosseum sat just behind us.

Theocoles squinted, looked all around, as Messalina and Bodhi continued to conference, the two of them whispering in a way that made me suspicious.

And I was so focused on watching them, that when Theocoles looked at me and said, "What can I expect when I get there?" well, I wasn't quite sure how to answer.

I took a moment to think about it, wondering how to best phrase it, just how much to reveal. I mean, I could give him a heads-up about the enlightening/mortifying life review process—I could tell him that he should definitely expect to be given an assignment of some kind—that it was nothing like the eternity of cloud lounging and harp lessons most people expect. But the more I thought about it, the more I realized that wasn't quite what he meant. Those weren't the kinds of details he was interested in.

He was worried about the choices he'd made—the way he'd lived his life. This was a guy who'd left heaps of slain bodies in the arena, and he was worried if he might somehow have to pay for all that.

And while I really had no idea either way, I was able to say, "All I know for sure is that you will be met with an abundance of compassion, love, and understanding." Remembering how I was the only one judging my actions in my own life review—I was the only one cringing at what I'd witnessed that day—the Council just wanted me to see my actions as clearly as they did.

Theocoles thought for a moment, then turning toward the Colosseum, he closed his eyes, threw his head back, and opened his arms wide, just like he did at each of his victories.

Though this time, it wasn't the sound of applause, or adoration, or any of the usual things that he sought—this time he listened much deeper, listened for the truth that lurked in his heart.

And when he was ready, when he gave his final nod of consent, I made the shimmering golden veil and waved him right through. Then I turned to Messalina, motioning for her to follow, only to have her shock me to the core when she made no move to join him.

"Messalina was not part of the assignment," Bodhi said, as though that explained it. "She is not ours to cross over."

The veil wavered before me, growing increasingly smaller with each passing second. "But what if she *wants* to cross over? You know, of her own free will? I mean, you *do* want to cross over, right? You've been waiting for this moment for over a thousand years!"

When her gaze shifted to Bodhi, I couldn't help but sigh. Couldn't help but turn away, my body strumming with anger as I thought: *Great. That's just great. Here we go again. Another gorgeous girl with a crush on my guide—get in line!*

I mean, seriously. Some love story that turned out to be. She swoons after Theocoles for centuries only to dump him at the veil the moment Bodhi with the green eyes arrives.

I felt like a sucker.

The most gullible ghost in the group.

I'd believed in her story—never once doubted their romance—and, as it turns out, it was as fake as the one I'd been engaged in.

"Not to worry," Bodhi said, trying to comfort me. "There's a whole group of people waiting for Theocoles, ready to help him get oriented, so don't worry about him, he'll be fine. And while Messalina will head over eventually, for now, there's been a slight change of plans . . ."

25

Although we ended up traveling a pretty sizeable distance, we chose not to fly.

Or rather, Bodhi and Messalina chose not to fly, Buttercup and I were forced to go along with it.

As it turns out, Messalina didn't know how to fly. And even though I offered to teach her (figuring if I could teach Buttercup, I could teach anyone), Bodhi was quick to quash it, claiming we had to hurry—that we didn't have time—and so we boarded a train instead.

I sulked by the window, spending the majority of the ride taking furtive peeks at Bodhi and Messalina, their heads ducked in whispers, paying no mind to me. And after about three and a half hours of steadily rolling down the tracks, the train finally came to a stop, and I was the first to leap up. Sighing and shaking my head as I made for the door, convinced that three and a half hours would've proved more than enough time to teach someone to fly.

And, as it turned out, three and a half hours was also enough time to travel from Rome to Venice.

Yep, Venice, Italy—home of canals, grand old waterfront palaces, and gondola rides—a city I'd always dreamed of visiting.

A city so beautiful I couldn't help but gasp as I struggled to take it all in.

A city so ripe with romance I couldn't help but notice the little pang of regret at my own lost romance, no matter how fake it might've been.

We stopped in the middle of St. Mark's Square, watching Buttercup drive himself bonkers by chasing after flocks of pigeons he couldn't quite catch. Barking, and growling, and flying and leaping, trying in vain to make contact, and yelping in confusion every time he ended up flying right through them instead.

"Is someone ever going to tell him he's dead?" I nodded toward my dog, knowing I was acting crabby, and grumpy, and worse, but I think I had good reason. Back in the Colosseum I'd acted nobly, heroically even. I'd willingly forfeited the Soul Catch to end all Soul Catches just so Messalina could be the master of her own happy ending—only to become a burdensome third wheel to their impromptu party. Someone they had no choice but to drag along for the ride.

"Listen, if you want to go on a gondola ride or something, feel free. Buttercup and I will wait here." I slumped to the ground, made myself comfortable, determined to make the best of a not so great situation, but still unable to stop myself from adding, "I mean, all I did was help Messalina snare the Soul Catch of the century—something I probably won't get any credit for—even though it was *my* idea—*my* words that awakened Theocoles. But hey, whatever, no biggie. I mean, it's not like I'm not used to it by now—in fact, I—"

Messalina looked at me, pressed a finger to her lips, and the gesture alone was enough to remind me.

I was doing it again.

Allowing myself to get lost in the soundtrack of my own sad story instead of what really, truly mattered—the fact that I was in Venice—something definitely worth celebrating. I mean, so what if they were planning to ditch me, at least I still had my dog.

"C'mere, Buttercup!" I patted my knees, laughing in hysterics when he came bounding toward me, leaping with such enthusiasm I fell to the ground, where I was instantly assaulted by a ridiculous amount of slobbery licks. "Alright already!" I laughed, pushing him away and getting him settled beside me. But only for a moment before he was up again, paws dancing wildly as he thrust his nose into the air and barked at something behind me. "What is it? What is it, boy?" I craned my neck, but still couldn't see what he saw.

"Why don't we go find out?" Bodhi said, motioning for us to follow as he traipsed down a maze of narrow, pedestrian-only alleyways, easing our way around hordes of tourists juggling armfuls of overflowing shopping bags, and slowing when we came to the door of a beautiful big old palace that butted right up against the water, as Bodhi waved us all through the locked door.

Buttercup sprinted ahead, barking in excitement as he tore up several flights of steep marble stairs, and it wasn't until I'd reached the landing that I heard it.

It was a song—one that could never be mistaken for anything other than what it was.

It was a song I knew well, in fact, it was one of my favorites.

It was the birthday song—and they were singing it for me.

I burst into the room—my face beaming, my eyes moving among the crowd—amazed to see everyone that mattered to me (well, everyone that mattered who was dead, anyway). Waving to my parents, my grandparents too, along with all the members of the Council, including: Royce, Claude, Celia, Samson, and Aurora (my not-so-secret favorite). Cheerleader Girl, also known as Jasmine, also known as

Bodhi's girlfriend, was there as well (probably more for Bodhi than me, but still, it was nice to see her). Even Mort, the guy who told me all about Dreamland, had dropped by, along with Balthazar, the director of Dreamland, who stood alongside him. And when my gaze landed on Prince Kanta, who I hadn't seen since my time on St. John, well, I couldn't help but squeal in delight. He'd brought Rebecca with him, and her little dog Shucky was already playing a game of Fetch with Buttercup. Even the Radiant Boys made an appearance (as it turned out, there were three), and I was happy to see that they'd ditched those gawd-awful little short sets they used to wear in favor of something way more contemporary. I mean, not that I cared—I was done judging people by their appearance (well, for the most part anyway). And while there were definitely a few people missing, namely the Weeping Woman, and Satchel the boy who makes nightmares, I decided not to focus on that.

Instead I focused on the song—and my friends—and the abundance of love and celebration that filled up the room. And when Bodhi stood before me holding a big, huge cake slathered in a thick coat of deep purple frosting—well, it seemed my birthday was complete.

"Corner piece is all yours—but only if you can blow out the candles in one breath," he said, grinning at me.

One breath—something that's a lot easier to accomplish when you're not dead.

I stared at the corner piece, the one with the big, sugary butterfly plunked down on its side, filling myself with great swallows of air, determined to nail it, and that's when I noticed something remarkable—the candles kept changing.

First there were thirteen.

Then there were fourteen.

Then fifteen.

Then back to thirteen again.

Once, it even went as low as twelve.

My gaze sought Aurora's, looking for answers (she always had answers), and she was quick to explain when she said, "The choice is yours. Just know that whichever age you choose, you have our full blessing. We are so proud of you, Riley, so proud of the unselfish choice you just made. You've come a very long way."

I gulped, returned my attention to the cake, and when it showed fifteen candles again, I thought: *Go! Do it! Then you can be equal with Bodhi! And then maybe he'll—*

But when I gazed at him again, I decided to let that one go. Some things just need to happen on their own. Some things cannot be forced.

Once I'd let fifteen go, it was easy to let fourteen go as well.

Been there—done that. And I knew with complete certainty that there was a really big difference between *looking* a certain age—and *feeling* a certain age.

I wasn't ready for the big time. Not even close.

Reminded of what Ever had said that time we met up in Dreamland—that I was lucky—that I wouldn't be forced into anything before I was ready—I would become a teen when the time was just right, not a moment earlier. And I had no doubt in my mind that my sister was right.

I'd been waiting to be thirteen for so long, I could hardly believe the moment had come.

But, I'd also had so much experience in the time since my death—I was no longer sure if it fit.

The candles flickered before me—adding—subtracting—over and over again.

And when my number finally appeared, I closed my eyes, sucked in a mouthful of air, and blew with all of my might.

Remembering to make a wish—you *always* have to make a wish.

And when I opened my eyes and looked down at myself, I saw that one of my wishes came true.

I wasn't just thirteen—I was thirteen and a half—*thankyouverymuch!*

It was an age I felt comfortable with—an age I'd earned—truly arrived at.

And, while my body was nowhere as impressive as it had been back in Rome, it also wasn't nearly as stick-figure-like anymore.

"If you wished for the corner piece, then your wish came true," Bodhi said, setting the cake on the table and carving me a big, hefty slice.

"Wouldn't you like to know?" I looked at him and rolled my eyes, but instead of that leading to a bickering session like it normally would, we both just cracked up.

Bodhi presented my piece and I was just about to dig in, when I remembered I wasn't the only one with a birthday to celebrate. So I closed my eyes long enough to manifest a beautiful cupcake topped with pink creamy frosting and dotted with little bits of candy that shimmered like jewels.

Then after plucking one of the candles from my cake, and sticking it in the middle of the cupcake, I looked at the crowd assembled before me and said, "Would you guys mind singing 'Happy Birthday' again? But this time, sing it to my friend, Messalina. She never had a birthday party, and it seems a bit overdue."

26

Even though I'd been waiting for it for years, even though I'd imagined it down to every last detail, as it turns out, my thirteenth birthday party wasn't at all like I'd thought.

Not just because I never imagined myself dead at thirteen.

Not just because I chose to tack on an additional six months by making myself thirteen and a half.

Not just because it technically wasn't a birthday party since it didn't take place on the day of my birth (I didn't know what day it was).

But mostly because for someone who'd spent most of my death feeling lonely and friendless, when I took in the crowd at my party, I realized I'd been anything but.

Okay, maybe I didn't know most of them all that well. Maybe a good amount of them were just people I worked with, people I once helped find their way to the Here &

Now. But still, I'd spent so much time feeling alone that I was blinded to the fact that there was actually a whole team of people cheering me on.

Unlike Theocoles, I'd tuned out their roar of approval for my own (mostly negative) thoughts. But no more—those days were over.

"Riley, this is amazing!" Messalina lifted her napkin, dabbed at a blob of frosting that had found its way to her chin. "Are birthdays always like this? If so, I can't wait to have another!"

"They're not always like this," I told her, jabbing my fork deep into a ball of sugary goodness. "But they should be." I took another bite and smiled, my teeth frosted with a thick coat of purple.

And that's when I saw him.

That's when I saw him gazing at me from across the room in much the same way he'd gazed at me the very first time at Messalina's never ending party.

With curiosity.

And intensity.

Along with a healthy dose of unmistakable interest.

Though unlike the last time, his usual surplus of confidence was lacking—along with his height, muscles, and overall level of maturity. (But he had ditched the fancy toga for jeans and a sweater, and that definitely worked in his favor.)

"He's real?" I turned to Messalina, my head swirling with

conflicting feelings of surprise and disbelief.

"He is indeed." Messalina smiled and leaned toward me, about to brush a crumb from my cheek, then thinking better of it, thinking I might think that she was trying to enchant me again, she settled for motioning toward it instead.

"So he wasn't just some soulless being you whipped into existence in order to keep me occupied?"

"Not even close. He truly was smitten the first moment he saw you, I had nothing to do with it."

"Was he—was he really a senator's son in his former life? Is that why he hung around for so long?" I bit down on my lip, wondering when he'd get the courage to cross the room and approach me.

Messalina shrugged. "Why don't you ask him yourself?"

I hesitated, not sure I could go through with it. It was a large room that seemed even larger when I remembered how different I must've looked from the girl he'd first fallen for—a girl who'd recently transformed from Aurelia Major back to Aurelia Minor.

"Why not try?" she nudged. "You'll never know until you try it, right?"

I sighed, figuring someone had to make the first move, so it may as well be me. Besides, the party provided the perfect excuse. I was just being a good hostess. Making sure he was having fun. That's all that it was. It didn't mean anything more.

I'd just screwed up my courage, just started to leave, when Messalina grabbed hold of my hand and pushed something hard and cool into the center of my palm. Then closing my fingers around it, she said, "I'll never forget the sacrifice you made on my behalf. You could've easily awakened Theocoles yourself, but instead, you gave the moment to me. I hope you'll decide to keep this small token of my appreciation, and maybe even wear it on occasion, if you like. It's a replica of the one that I wear." She lifted her hand, wiggled her finger so that her ring caught the light. "Think of it as a symbol of our friendship. We may not be sisters, but I hope we'll be friends."

I slipped the ring onto my finger and held it up beside hers, deciding to keep it, to wear it every day. I liked the way that it looked, sure, but more importantly I liked the idea of having a friend so close we were almost related.

"And Theocoles?" My eyes met hers.

"I'm headed there now." She smiled. "That is if you can make the veil for me, please?"

I closed my eyes long enough to envision the shimmering golden veil that would lead her to Summerland, the bridge, and the world just beyond where she would join Theocoles.

And once that was done, once I waved her right through, I set off on my own journey—crossing the room to where Dacian stood.

27

The moment I stood before Dacian, the first thing I thought was: *Wow, he's changed even more than I thought!*

The second thing was: *But he's still cute. Like, super, big-time cute—and he looks to be my age as well—what a relief!*

So what if he wasn't as confident?

So what if he wasn't nearly as noble and old-fashioned as he was when I met him?

I, for one, was glad when instead of taking my hand and bowing to kiss it—he just gave a little wave and said, "Hey."

But that's probably because he wasn't really the son of a Roman senator who hung around the last several centuries unwilling to let go of his old life. That was just a role he'd found himself playing.

Turns out, he was a Soul Catcher like me.

"Seriously?" I could hardly believe it, could hardly contain my excitement. I didn't know any other Soul

Catchers beside Bodhi, and I couldn't help but be thrilled by the news, knowing it gave us something in common.

He nodded in a way that caused his hair to fall into his eyes, looking more than a little embarrassed to admit it. "Did you really believe I was a bona fide toga wearer?"

I nodded, laughing when I said, "Yeah, or at least at first anyway. Later I decided you were a fake."

He squinted, unsure what to make of that.

"You know how Messalina manifested all of those party guests? Well, I thought you were one of them. I thought you were soulless. I was sure she whipped you into existence just to keep me occupied." I shrugged. "Anyway, how long were you stuck?"

He sighed, looked away, shoved his hands deep into his pockets, and said, "A really, really long time. Or at least it feels that way, it's hard to be sure."

"And, what was it that unstuck you?" I asked. I hadn't seen it happen, and I truly was curious.

Had the world been dissolved when Theocoles and Messalina left it—or did it continue? Were other Soul Catchers still roaming around that sad, horrible place, lost in a long-ago past? Now that I'd completed my mission, I might never know.

My thoughts interrupted by the sound of him saying, "You."

I cocked my head, thinking surely I hadn't heard him quite right.

But before he had a chance to repeat it, Bodhi joined us and said, "A bunch of us are going for gondola rides, you guys interested?"

I looked at Dacian and he looked at me, the two of us blurting, "Okay!" at the exact same time, in the exact same way, and we couldn't help but burst out in laughter.

Bodhi glanced between, his eyes containing a glint of something I couldn't quite read. "Great," he said. "You guys can share with us, the gondola should easily fit five, including Buttercup."

And though I was still excited by the idea of a gondola ride, I couldn't help but stare at him with suspicion.

Bodhi never wanted to spend time with me.

In fact, it was more like the opposite. He was always trying to ditch me so he could be with his girlfriend. And with my birthday party winding down, I had a hard time believing that he really wanted to hang around with me, and Dacian, and my dog, when he could be exploring one of the most romantic cities in the world with Jasmine.

"I just thought it would be fun," Bodhi said, his hand waving before him, reacting to the skeptical look on my face when he added, "But, maybe not. No worries, we'll just grab our own."

He turned, started to leave, when a new thought occurred to me: *Maybe Bodhi wasn't trying to supervise me,*
spy on me, or keep tabs on me. Maybe he was just trying to
be friendly, get to know me, spend a little time outside of Soul
Catching to have a little fun, now that I was a teenager and
we were closer in age. Maybe I'd gotten so used to not having
friends, I didn't know how to act when I did.

"Wait!" I stepped forward, grabbed ahold of his sleeve.
"I'd love to share with you guys—I think it sounds fun." I
nodded, anxious for him to know that I meant what I said.

Turning to Dacian, making sure it was okay with him, a
flush of heat rising to my cheeks when he nodded, grasped
my hand in his, and laced our fingers loosely together.

A move that was not lost on Bodhi as his eye darted
between Dacian and me, his brow quirking, thoughts
swirling, as he said, "What do you say we *vamanos* then,
boat's waiting!"

We left the gorgeous Venetian palace in one long procession—a long stream of ghosts slipping through an old locked
door before wandering down a maze of narrow alleyways to
the place where those long, curving boats were all docked.

My progress halted when Bodhi turned and grabbed
hold of my arm, telling Dacian and Jasmine to continue, that

we'd catch up soon enough, then he pulled me into a small boutique as he said, "There's something I want you to see."

I stared at him in confusion, having no idea what he was getting at. I mean, yeah, the dresses they sold were all very pretty, but I had no need for shopping when I could just manifest whatever new clothes I might want. Besides, I liked what I wore, I'd been through so many changes already, I wasn't really looking for any more.

But when he pushed me before a full-length mirror and said, "Look," I did.

Taking in a blond ponytail, bright blue eyes, cheek-bones that were a little more pronounced than I was used to (which in turn made my nose slightly less semi-stubby!), and yeah, instead of caving like it usually did, the top part of my T-shirt actually jutted out.

Okay, maybe *jutted out* isn't exactly accurate—maybe it's a bit of an exaggeration. But what I can say for sure is that for the first time ever the fabric didn't cave in. And yeah, seeing that made me feel proud.

But, as it turns out that's not what Bodhi was referring to. He was pointing to my glow.

"Why'd you get rid of it?" He peered hard at me, wanting to understand why I'd do such a thing when my glow once meant so much to me.

"I wanted to fit in." I shrugged, my gaze roving my

reflection in wonder. "And no one in Messalina's world had one. But also, to be honest, the way that it dimmed after what happened in Dreamland only reminded me of how bad I screwed up—how far I still had to go."

"And now?" Bodhi's voice was quiet and gentle, but nudging as well.

"And now it seems I'm well on my way." I grinned, taking in my solid green glow, noting how it was much like the color Bodhi's had been the day we first met—the day he first became my guide—an act that had changed the course of my afterlife.

Thanks to Messalina, I'd gotten a good long glimpse of the future. I'd seen firsthand just what I was capable of. Bodhi had too. And while I had no idea just when that future would unfold, I knew that it would. Of that I was sure.

The only thing that had changed was my hurry to get there. I was no longer sprinting toward it. Instead I decided to enjoy each day as it comes. Like they said in ancient Rome: *Carpe diem!*

"Are you happy?" Bodhi asked, and when I looked into his eyes, I knew better than to answer flippantly, or worse—shrug it off. It was clear just how very serious his question really was.

I paused, taking a moment to arrange my thoughts. Wavering between saying something deeply profound versus keeping it simple. But before I could get there, Buttercup ran into the store, clamped down on my pant leg, and yanked hard with his teeth.

"Boats are all waiting—you two still coming?" Jasmine glanced between us, her face betraying a small hint of worry.

I nodded, laughing as I allowed Buttercup to haul me outside to where Dacian waited. His hand closing around mine as I glanced over my shoulder, my eyes meeting Bodhi's when I said, "Yes. The answer to your question is *yes*. I've never been happier."

Author's Note

While the characters and the situations they find themselves in are fictional, the ruins of the Ludus Magnus, thought to be the most important gladiatorial training school of the time, exist to this day. The restaurant that overlooks it is also real. However, I've taken significant liberties with the layout of the *ludus* and its history in order to fit the needs of the story.